Inherited: One Child

DAY LECLAIRE

First published in Great Britain 2010
Large Print edition 2010
Harlequin Mills & Boon Limited,
Eton House, 18-24 Paradise Road,
Richmond, Surrey TW9 1SR

© Day Totton Smith 2009

ISBN: 978 0 263 21574 8

Printed and bound in Great Britain
by CPI Antony Rowe, Chippenham, Wiltshire

DAY LECLAIRE

is a three-time winner of both the Colorado Award of Excellence and the Golden Quill Award. She's won *RT Book Reviews* magazine's Career Achievement and Love and Laughter awards, the Holt Medallion, a Bookseller's Best Award, and has received an impressive ten nominations for the prestigious Romance Writers of America RITA® Award. Day's romances touch the heart and make you care about her characters as much as she does. In Day's own words, "I adore writing romances, and can't think of a better way to spend each day." For more information, visit Day on her website, www.dayleclaire.com.

To the four-legged wonders
who share our lives and give us
such unstinting love and devotion.
To those who have come and gone…
Yoson and Brutus,
Little John and Thursday,
and Annie.

And those who give us daily joy…
Yoda and Ruggy, Athena and Guinness

Prologue

"**Y**ou have no choice, Jack. If you want to keep custody of Isabella, you're going to have to marry."

Jack Mason glared at his lawyer. "You know I swore I never would."

Derek dismissed that with a wave of his hand. "So you've said. Ad nauseam, I might add."

"Then let's move on, shall we? What's my next option?"

"Jack, I'm telling you flat out. There is no

other choice." Derek leaned a hip against his desk while Jack prowled the length of the office. "Look, we've been friends since our college days. You may not have told me all that went on between your parents, but having met your father, I can guess. That doesn't change the facts. CPS is very concerned about your niece, thanks to that psychologist's report."

"I wish I could call the man a liar." Jack thrust a hand through his hair and blew out his breath in a long sigh. "But he was simply stating the facts. It's been three months since the plane crash and Isabella isn't adjusting at all. Her tantrums have escalated. And she's still not speaking."

Sympathy lined Derek's dark face. "Providing your niece with a stable home life and continuing with therapy will go a long way toward changing that."

"I've hired nannies for her." Jack could hear the defensive edge in his voice and fought to eradicate it. Getting ticked off at the one person squarely on his side wasn't his best strategy. "I have a business empire to run, Derek. Isabella is only five. I can't be her caretaker 24/7."

"Child Protective Services is well aware that you've had an endless stream of nannies since March. According to the letter I've received, they're not happy about it. And frankly, Jack, it's not helping with Isabella's recovery." Derek hesitated. "There is another alternative."

Jack lifted an eyebrow. "Go on."

"Let her go. You can afford to find a good home for her. The best possible home. A home with two parents. Someone who has the time to commit to Isabella's well-being."

"I can't do that." The words were ripped from him, low and guttural. "I won't."

Derek didn't bother to pull his punches. "That's your guilt talking. Isabella survived the plane crash and your sister and brother-in-law didn't. You also believe you should have been on that plane with them."

Jack couldn't deny it, not when it was the

truth. "I was supposed to be. If I had been… If I hadn't let work delay me…"

"You'd most likely be dead, too, and Isabella would be in the exact same position she is now," Derek stated with brutal logic. "In need of two stable parents who can give their full attention to her needs—something you aren't in a position to do."

"I won't desert her." Jack continued to pace the width of his office while frustration ate at him. "I just need to find the right person. It's taking a bit longer than expected."

"You need a wife. The caseworker is old-school, Jack. And she's from the north. She doesn't care how much money you have or what your name is, or whether your ancestors were among the first residents of Charleston. Her only concern is Isabella."

Jack shot his friend a black look. "And mine isn't?"

Derek's expression softened. "I know you care about your niece. But you've seen her exactly twice since Joanne adopted her, both times when she was little more than a baby. You have no blood ties. You're a stranger to her. And ever since the psychologist released his evaluation, Mrs. Locke has made it clear that she doesn't consider you a suitable guardian. She's actually mentioned placing Isabella in a treatment facility."

Stark fury gripped him. "Over my dead body."

"You won't have any choice in the matter. They'll simply come and take Isabella from you—by force, if necessary." Derek took a seat behind his desk and released a sigh. "What happened, Jack? You were supposed to talk to Mrs. Locke. *Sweet*-talk her, to be precise."

Jack grimaced. "There isn't sufficient sugar on earth to sweeten up that woman."

"You should have made more of an effort, instead of throwing her out of your office. Her opinion will carry a lot of weight in court, as will the psychologist's findings."

"Are you saying that ticking her off wasn't my best business decision?" Jack asked drily. When his friend maintained a diplomatic silence, he allowed the moment to stretch while he considered his options. Not that there were many. "What if I do what you suggest and marry?" The words grated like ground glass in his mouth.

"Then you have a real shot at retaining custody, assuming the Locke woman believes the marriage is genuine. I strongly recommend you choose a bride who has experience dealing with special-needs children. A teacher or a social worker. A do-gooder type who will devote all her time to Isabella's welfare."

"Just like that? Find a do-gooder and marry her." Jack folded his arms across his chest. "And how do you propose I accomplish such an amazing feat?"

"I recommend you find her the same way you found your nannies. You advertise."

Jack stared in disbelief. "You want me to advertise for a wife?"

"No, I want you to advertise for a nanny and

then marry her. You find a woman you can live with until CPS signs off on the case, and I'll draw up an ironclad prenup."

Jack had never considered himself slow on the uptake. But this left him totally at sea. "How the blue blazes am I supposed to convince the woman to marry me? Lie to her? Trick her? Pretend I'm madly in love with her?"

Derek shrugged. "If you want. Personally, I'd recommend a far simpler method."

"Which is?"

"Hell, Jack. How many billions do you have moldering away in various financial institutions? Even I've lost track. Take a healthy chunk of it and buy the damn woman."

One

Jack Mason knew he was in trouble the minute he saw her.

He didn't know why she snagged his attention, considering she sat in a room crowded with nanny applicants of all shapes, colors and ages, none of whom possessed a clue about his true intentions—choosing one of them for his wife. This woman dressed in a somber black pantsuit that wasn't the least eye-catching, so perhaps his reaction had something to do with the way she sat reading a paperback novel...perfectly composed and preternaturally still, an expression of absolute patience on a face more striking than beautiful.

Jack examined her with greater care. Interesting. Everything about her appeared quiet and understated. She'd pulled her hair into ruthless obedience, anchoring the ebony mass into a tight knot at her nape. In addition, she'd used a restrained hand with her makeup, just a hint of color on her cheeks and lips. A light brush of taupe across her eyelids drew attention to a startling pair of deep-set eyes that wavered somewhere between honey and gold and were framed by lush black lashes. She looked impossibly young, and yet one glimpse of those eyes warned of someone who'd been through the pits of hell and back again. They overflowed with ancient wisdom and intense vulnerability.

Was that why he'd keyed in on her from all those crowding the room? And what, in particular, about her appearance aroused such intense interest? It was something subtle. Something that stirred instincts he'd honed during his years surviving in the shark-infested waters of the business world. Those instincts warned that this woman, while appearing so calm and controlled on the outside, seethed with secret passion. It was almost as though he sensed the ebb and flow of those restless seas and reacted on a visceral level to a call only he could hear.

If they'd met anywhere else, he'd have moved in on her and cut her from the crowd. He'd have found a way to break through that carefully cultivated self-control and release the inner passion. It had always been that way with him. He'd always responded to the essence of the woman swirling beneath the surface and felt the burning need to strip her down, layer by layer, to that passionate inner core.

This woman would have many layers, fascinating layers. Layers he could explore intellectually and physically. And he wanted to develop—wanted with an intensity he hadn't experienced in years.

One of his prospective "wives" coughed, snapping Jack's concentration. Awareness of time and place returned, along with an irritation that he'd allowed such pointless speculation to distract him. He forced his attention back to the business at hand—securing a woman who could act the part of both nanny and wife. On the verge of calling the next name on the list, the door to the outer office flew open and his niece burst in.

Her short, curly hair stood out from her head in matted golden-brown spikes that had yet to see a brush that morning, and he could tell what she'd eaten for breakfast with a single look at her shirt. She'd worked a hole into each knee of her new jeans—with a pair of scissors, by the look of it. And she'd used her watercolor paints to turn her face into a startling mask of red and black swirls.

Isabella scanned the room in frantic anger, her olive green eyes narrowed to slits. Taking a stance dead center in the room, she balled her hands into fists and then opened her mouth, letting out a scream loud and shrill enough to cause the windowpanes in his office to shiver in protest. For a split second, everyone in the outer room froze. Jack considered taking control of the situation, but then decided to wait and see how his nanny applicants reacted.

Some of the women took decisive action. They bolted for the door. Jack sighed. Three down. Several of the others exchanged uneasy glances, clearly uncertain how to respond to the crazed child who'd erupted into their midst. One large-set, no-nonsense woman rose and approached Isabella.

"You stop that this instant," she demanded.

Isabella responded by kicking the woman in the shin and increasing the volume and shrill- ness of her screaming, something Jack would have thought an impossibility. But somehow, his darling niece managed it. The woman exited, muttering furiously beneath her breath—four down—and Jack thanked his lucky stars. He didn't think he could handle a wife with a moustache. Nor did he think Mrs. Locke would believe theirs was a real marriage.

Successfully having rid herself of four of the applicants, Isabella took control of the room. She darted from person to person, giving them an exclusive, one-on-one performance. Each reacted differently. Some attempted to cajole. Others took the first woman's approach and made demands. One actually threatened Isabella with a spanking. Several made shushing noises. Only the woman in black didn't react. She continued to sit quietly, reading her book as though she neither saw nor heard the chaos exploding around her. Isabella took note and her jaw assumed a determined slant.

Jack winced. Hell.

Rushing over to stand in front of the woman, Isabella gave full throttle to her displeasure. It didn't make a bit of difference. The only response was a leisurely turn of the page. Finally, Isabella's voice gave out and she croaked into silence. Only then did the woman look up. For an instant the two stared at each other, a silent contest of wills.

An odd expression burned in the woman's eyes, something that might have been fear combined with an intense vulnerability, which didn't bode well for her ability to control a child of Isabella's willful nature. In the next moment, the look vanished, replaced by a gentle relentlessness, a searing look of hope combined with determination. The expression took his breath away. She'd only been in Isabella's presence for mere moments, and yet he could practically see her weaving an emotional connection with his niece.

She said something to Isabella in a voice so soft it didn't carry any farther than his niece's ears. Then she stood and walked to the door. Opening it, she scanned the area. "Who's in charge of this child?" Jack heard her ask.

The temporary babysitter he'd hired, who'd no doubt been cowering in the hallway, reluctantly stepped forward. "I am."

Without another word, the woman ushered Isabella through the door and, before the child could react, closed it decisively in her face. Then she returned to her seat, picked up her book and resumed reading. A scattering of applause broke out around her, not that she took any notice. Even so, Jack could tell the incident had affected her. A telltale pulse throbbed at the base of her throat, betraying her agitation. It impressed the hell out of him that she could hide her reaction so well. He checked his watch and grimaced. Time to move this show along.

He called the next name on the list. "Annalise Stefano."

He wasn't the least surprised when the woman he'd been studying tucked away her book, shouldered her purse and stood. Somehow, the name fit. She walked toward him with a long, easy stride that suited her lean, coltish build. A tiny curl sprang loose from the tight control she'd attempted to impose on it and bounced against her temple in joyful exuberance. He almost smiled. Her hair was one of the layers he'd love to peel away. How would she look with all those curls tumbling down her back in total abandon?

"I'm Annalise," she said, and offered her hand. "It's a pleasure to meet you, Mr. Mason."

He took her hand in his and felt the odd dichotomy of fine bones in opposition to a tensile strength. Did it reflect the woman? He suspected it did. He forced himself to release her, when in truth he experienced a sharp desire to tug her closer, if only to see how she'd react, to see how deep that self-control ran. Not good. Whomever he chose for this job would be his temporary wife, a woman he'd want out of his life as soon as feasible. That meant their relationship could be boiled down to two words.

Hands. Off.

"Ms. Stefano," he said. "Come with me." He started to close the door to his office and caught a glimpse of another of the applicants scurrying toward the exit. Hell. Five down, though at least it was the one who'd advocated spanking. He closed the door and waved a hand toward one of the two chairs in front of his desk. "Have a seat while I review your résumé."

He scanned it quickly to refresh his memory. Right, right. He remembered this one. He'd almost rejected her out of hand because she had so little practical experience. What had tipped the scales in her favor was the fact that she'd received her teaching certificate in early childhood and elementary education, as well as in special ed, and that she'd possessed glowing recommendations. They were right in line with the qualifications Derek recommended in his future bride.

"I assume my assistant explained why I'm in need of a nanny?"

"Yes, she did. I also read about the tragedy in the newspapers, Mr. Mason. I'm very sorry for your loss."

He inclined his head, relieved that he didn't

have to go into lengthy explanations. The papers had been quite thorough in that regard. "I'm afraid you had the pleasure of meeting my niece, Isabella, a few minutes ago."

Annalise offered a quick smile, one that transformed her face, lifting it from striking to luminescent. "So I gathered."

"As you can see, she's having a difficult time making the transition." He held out his hands. "And who can blame her? Not only did she lose her parents three months ago, but she's been uprooted from her home in Colorado."

Sympathy radiated off Annalise and her eyes glittered with a wealth of emotion. "That explains a lot about her current behavior."

Jack inclined his head. "When she first came to live with me, I contacted an agency to hire a qualified daytime caregiver. I went through their entire portfolio the first month. The longest stayed a week. The shortest clocked in at just under an hour. Since then, I've decided to take matters into my own hands and hire someone myself. Which brings me to your application, Ms. Stefano."

"Please call me Annalise."

"Fine. Annalise it is." He paused on the first page of her application. "You're qualified to teach elementary school. Why have you applied for a position as a nanny?"

She didn't hesitate, clearly anticipating the question. "I'm interested in attaining my master's before taking on a teaching job. This position will provide me with more flexibility than teaching and fewer hours of preparation while I pursue that goal."

He tilted his head to one side. That would fit in with his own plans. She could pursue her master's program—a program he'd be only too happy to pay for—while playing the role of devoted wife and mother. "Would you be willing to commit to an employment contract of two full years? And would you be willing to homeschool Isabella, if needed?"

She folded her hands in her lap and met his

gaze dead-on. "It will take me two years to complete my master's program, so that aspect isn't a problem. Since it's the end of the school year right now, your niece and I will have the summer to work out a comfortable routine before fall classes begin. If you want to initiate a schooling program for her at that point, I'll have the next few months to put together a curriculum that meets with your approval. Then I can implement Isabella's lessons while I begin evening classes toward my master's."

Despite her outer calm, he sensed a certain level of nervousness—almost anxiety—and couldn't help but wonder what caused it. He allowed the silence to drag while he considered the various reasons for her turmoil. She could be nervous because she was lying to him about something, in which case he'd find a way to get to the truth. The irony of that fact didn't escape him, considering this entire interview was a huge fraud. Even so, he needed to trust his future wife, which meant all the cards on the table. Of course, she could be nervous because she didn't handle interviews well. One other possibility occurred to him, one that caused his gut to tighten and an unwanted hunger to gnaw at him.

Maybe *he* made her uneasy. Maybe she'd experienced the same odd awareness that he had. She didn't break the lengthy silence with a rush of nervous explanations the way many would have. That fact alone impressed the hell out of him.

"Let me be frank, Annalise. I'm concerned that you may change your mind midsummer and take a teaching position, leaving me to go through this process all over again. Isabella's had enough trauma and loss in her life without experiencing another so soon."

"That won't happen."

Instinct told him that she spoke with absolute sincerity. Even so, he sensed an intense emotional current that continued to ripple just beneath the surface, though he still couldn't quite pinpoint the reason for it. Perhaps it was a simple case of interview jitters. He glanced down at her file.

"I see you've also had some training with special-needs."

She stilled in the act of brushing another loosened curl away from her eyes. Her expression grew troubled. "Has Isabella always been a special-needs child? Or is today's incident related to the plane crash?"

He hesitated, choosing his words with care. "It started after she came to live with me. I want to make sure I hire someone who can help her adjust. Frankly, I don't think you have the necessary experience."

"Is she seeing a counselor?"

"I don't have much choice in the matter. CPS has insisted."

She raised an eyebrow at his dry tone. "With good reason. Children of that age can be manipulative. If she feels like you're cutting her some slack because of her loss, she'll use that for as long as it works. You should also consider talking to one yourself in order to learn how to best provide for her needs."

He leaned back in his chair and lifted an eyebrow. "Do I look like the sort of man who can be easily manipulated? Or is it just that you don't think I can provide for her needs?"

"Look, I'm not saying you can't or shouldn't give her love and stability and reassurance. I'm just suggesting you don't allow pity to make you too indulgent." Then she grinned, the vibrant flash of it arrowing straight through to his gut. "And now I've moved from dispensing unwanted advice to lecturing. It's well-intentioned, honestly."

He knew it, just as he knew it was advice identical to that of the psychologists he'd consulted. "How would you deal with her temper tantrums? If I hire you, you won't be able to do what you did a few moments ago and hand Isabella off to someone else. Next time you'll be the one in charge."

"I'll try a variation on what I did today. Ignore her screaming when practical, making sure she can't injure herself. Remove her from the situation when necessary, particularly if we're in public. Afterward, talk to her in a calm fashion and make it clear that her behavior is unacceptable. In time, when she doesn't get the response she's hoping for, she should stop." She offered a wry smile. "Of course, then she'll try something else."

Curiosity filled him. "What did you say to her before you put her out?"

"I told her that screaming is unacceptable behavior, and that there are consequences when she chooses to resort to a tantrum."

"What sort of consequences?" His eyes narrowed. "Do you believe in spanking?"

"No, I don't," she retorted crisply. "Do you?"

A smile loosened his mouth before he could prevent it. "No."

"That's a relief."

"So, if you don't utilize corporal punishment, then how do you plan to change her behavior?"

He was genuinely curious, since none of the methods he'd attempted had worked. Of course, he had not been consistent, nor had he been Isabella's main caregiver except for those first weeks immediately after the plane crash. Right on the heels of her release from the hospital, his work obligations had taken up most of his time, limiting the hours he spent with her. Plus, he doubted the interim sitters he'd employed had helped the situation. There hadn't been any consistency in his parenting and it showed.

"Is she intelligent?"

"Highly."

Annalise nodded. "She needs to be challenged intellectually, as well as physically, in order to help her stress level. In other words, she needs to engage in activities that will allow her to cope with her grief and confusion and work through them at her own pace. It would help to have a daily schedule that doesn't vary, so she knows that every day she gets up at the same time, eats at the same time, goes to bed at the same time, all of which gives her a feeling of security."

"She doesn't have that right now."

Annalise lifted a shoulder in an expressive shrug. "Because she's so young she may not be able to verbalize her fears and concerns. It would help to find creative outlets that allow for that expression. Painting or coloring, games that require organization, regular exercise, other children she can socialize with so she can just be a quote-unquote child for a while." She paused. "Does she have nightmares?"

"Yes."

Annalise nodded, as though not surprised. "She may also revert to behaviors she exhibited at a far younger age, such as thumb-sucking or bed-wetting."

"I haven't noticed any of that, so far." Well, except for one not-so-minor detail that he'd neglected to mention—her refusal to speak.

Annalise leaned forward. "As I said, continuing with a counselor is vital. He can help you and Isabella's main caregiver develop some strategies to assist in her recovery."

Annalise was right and he knew it. He glanced down at his list of questions and moved on to less complicated issues. "I'm sure my assistant mentioned that this job is five days a week, daytime shift."

"Will you be hiring a nighttime caregiver?"

"I did that right after I brought Isabella home from the hospital. Mrs. Walters will arrive at the end of your shift and cover until I get home. She also stays overnight when I'm out of town on business. If I needed you on an occasional night, would that be a problem?"

"Not at all."

So far, so good. He tapped a finger on the list of questions and moved on to the next issue. "Do you have a first-aid certificate?"

"Yes, as well as a criminal-convictions certificate."

He flipped through the file until he found

them. The first-aid certificate was recent and, as expected, she didn't have a criminal record. "Do you have any problem with my running a background check?" The slightest hesitation combined with a hint of worry passed over her features. His gaze narrowed. "Problem?" he asked coldly.

She shook her head. "No, I can see where you'd need to do that. I'd just appreciate some time so I can warn my friends and relatives."

"Warn?"

She sighed. "Alert. Is that a better word for it? I'd like to call them first and ask for their cooperation, so they're not taken by surprise."

"Fair enough." If she really was hiding anything, his private investigator would find it. He moved on. "Do you smoke?"

"No."

"Are you involved in an intimate relationship?"

Again, she hesitated. "How is that germane?"

He studied her curiously, wondering if he'd hit

on something. "I need to know if you have any obligations that may interfere with your ability to give Isabella your full attention." Or prevent her from becoming his temporary wife. "I also need to know about anyone who may come into regular contact with my niece so that I can have them checked out."

"Of course." She inclined her head and another curl escaped, this one just behind her left ear. The shiny black ringlet bounced against the long line of her neck, providing an irritating distraction. "No, to answer your question, I'm not in an intimate relationship."

He lifted an eyebrow. "What about a casual relationship?"

A hint of color marched along the sculpted curve of her cheekbones. "I'm not in any sort of relationship at all."

He fought the satisfaction her response elicited. "How do you get along with your family?"

He'd caught her by surprise again. "There's just my father, and we get along fine."

"How often do you see him?"

Her brow puckered in bewilderment. "Once a week. Sometimes more often, now that I'm back in South Carolina."

"Does he live in Charleston?"

"Jim Isle, born and bred."

"How much contact do you anticipate he'll have with Isabella?"

To his surprise, a flash of alarm flickered through her eyes, darkening the honey gold to a deep amber. "I...I don't anticipate there being any contact between them."

He digested that for a moment. "Why not?" he finally asked.

She floundered for an instant. It was the first time he'd seen a serious crack in her composure and it filled him with curiosity. "Because my time with Isabella is business related and the time I spend with my father is personal. I really don't see the two crossing paths."

Interesting. "You believe in keeping your work and home life separate?"

"Don't you?" When he didn't respond to the question, she brushed it aside with a fleeting wave of her hand. "Yes, I prefer to keep the two parts of my life separate."

"Is there some reason you don't want your father to come into contact with Isabella? Does he have a criminal record? Would he be a bad influence on a child?"

"No," she instantly denied. "Not at all. My father is a good man. I just prefer to keep my family life private. Is that a problem for you?"

"I have no objection either way."

Surprise swept across her face, followed by relief, before she masked her emotions behind a facade of calm serenity. It was an interesting transformation to watch. He suspected her exquisite self-control was an innate part of her personality, and he couldn't help wondering what circumstances had occurred in her life that had required her to develop this ability. Had she also experienced trauma? Was that why she shrouded herself in unruffled composure, as a way to combat the whirlwind of strife and turmoil?

He took a quick stab in the dark. "You mention your father, but not your mother."

She took a quick breath. "My mother died when I was twelve."

"A difficult age to lose a mother."

A dry smile kicked up the corner of her mouth. "Is there a good age?"

"No. Even so... You must have learned coping mechanisms."

"Eventually."

"Would any of them help Isabella?"

"Some." She considered briefly. "In theory."

"Why in theory?"

"Because Isabella isn't me," she explained. "What worked for one person might not work for another. It's not a one-size-fits-all."

He leaned back in his chair and studied her for a long moment. He was tempted to hire her. So very, very tempted. Again, he sensed a ripple of tension just beneath her calm expression.

"You've met Isabella. You see how much work it's going to take to get through to her. Why do you want this job so badly?"

Annalise moistened her lips and answered with care. "Isabella needs help. Maybe I can give her that help. At the very least I'll find out whether I'm capable of handling special-needs children."

"I'm not sure I want to hire someone who regards this as an experiment or a test of their capabilities." She didn't respond to the observation, though he could tell his comment worried her. "There's one other detail you should know about Isabella."

"Which is?"

He decided to lay it out for her. If it scared her off, he'd know she was wrong for the job. "After we explained what happened to her parents, my niece stopped speaking."

Annalise inhaled sharply. "She doesn't talk? Not at all?"

"She screams. That's her communication of

choice. So you can see why I'd like the most experienced person possible for this job."

"Yes, I can understand that," she conceded. "But I'd still like a shot at the position."

Jack released his breath in a slow sigh. There were two reasons he didn't plan to hire Annalise Stefano, despite the urge to do just that. The first and most important was that she didn't have the necessary experience. Good instincts, but little hands-on practice. What if Mrs. Locke decided Annalise wasn't knowledgeable enough? He'd have precisely one shot at this. If the caseworker gave the thumbs-down, he couldn't run out and find a replacement bride. No, whoever he chose would have to be as close to perfect as possible.

The second reason he hesitated was the attraction he felt toward Annalise. It didn't bode well for a successful working relationship and threatened unending complications down the road. Plus, it didn't make sense to keep such blatant temptation in his home. Too risky.

He flipped the file closed. "I appreciate you coming in for this interview."

She fought to maintain her composure. "You've already made up your mind, haven't you?" A dark, husky note slipped into her voice and he gained the impression that she'd pinned a lot of hopes on this job. "You're not going to hire me." It wasn't a question.

"I'm sorry, Ms. Stefano." He let her down as gently as possible. "You've only just completed your studies. You haven't had any practical experience. I need someone who's actually worked with children like Isabella."

She didn't argue, although he suspected she wanted to. "If you change your mind, you have my number." She stood and approached his desk, holding out her hand. "Thank you for considering me, Mr. Mason."

He took her hand again, experiencing that same oddly appealing dichotomy of strength overlaying fragility. Of vulnerability warring with quiet determination. He didn't doubt she'd have thrown her heart and soul into helping Isabella, and he couldn't help but wonder if he was making a horrible mistake in not choosing her. He deliberately quashed any doubts. Doubts equaled weakness, and he learned at his father's knee never to allow weakness to influence a business decision.

Releasing Annalise's hand, he picked up the list of applicants and escorted her to the door. He opened it and froze. The outer office was deserted. Not a single person remained.

"Well, hell."

Annalise planted her hands on her hips and surveyed the empty chairs. "I don't suppose you'd care to reconsider that job offer?"

What choice did he have? Time was of the essence and Annalise had come close—very, very close—to fitting the profile he needed for both a nanny and a wife. "As a matter of fact, I would like to reconsider."

She nodded. "I thought you might." Her brilliant smile transformed her appearance once again. "When would you like me to start?"

In the distance, a shriek of anger penetrated the walls. Jack released an exhausted sigh. "Is now too soon?"

"That depends."

He regarded her warily. "On what?"

"Before I give you my answer, I'd like to get the opinion of one of the top businessmen in the country." She slanted him a teasing glance. "Would this be a good time to ask for a raise?"

Nothing about the events of today were funny, and yet he found himself grinning, anyway. "I'm sorry to say that now would be an excellent time." He waved her back toward the chair in front of his desk. "Why don't you make yourself comfortable while we discuss an early-start bonus."

Two

Mary opened the door to Jack's office and regarded him with sympathetic eyes. "Ms. Stefano has asked to see you," his assistant informed him. "Sorry, boss."

He checked his watch. His brand-new nanny-slash-prospective-wife-to-be had lasted all of thirty minutes. He'd hoped for longer, but he was a realistic man. Isabella had driven away the best of the best. What chance did someone with Annalise's lack of experience stand?

"Does she have Isabella with her?"

"No. She requested that the babysitter stay. He's keeping an eye on your niece for the moment."

Jack sighed. "Send her in."

Annalise appeared a moment later, entering with that loose, hip-swing stride he found so attractive. More curls had escaped the tidy knot, bubbling down her back and around her face in gay abandon. Her startling eyes, now a darker shade of honey-gold, were tarnished with concern.

"Mr. Mason—"

"Might as well make it Jack."

She nodded impatiently. "This isn't working, Jack."

"I have to admit. You disappoint me." He leaned back in his chair and drummed his fingers against the leather armrest. "You also win the prize for shortest nanny on record."

She froze, blinking her long sooty lashes at him. "Shortest—" Her breath exploded in a short laugh. "No, you don't understand. I'm not quitting. I'd like to get Isabella out of here. We need to work together one-on-one away from your office. If we're going to establish a routine, we should do that right from the start." She lifted an eyebrow. "Unless you intend for us to come in and disrupt your work every day?"

"Of course not." He checked his watch and frowned. "I was planning to take you home at lunchtime."

Annalise shook her head. "That won't work. There's too much going on here, too much excitement. It's getting Isabella riled up. We should leave now, and then I need you to sit quietly with her for a time and explain who and what I am. It would help with the transition."

Jack frowned. "You haven't already done that?"

He caught her unexpected flash of temper before she reined it in. "You're her uncle, which makes you the authority figure," she explained. "Isabella needs you to organize her world and then set the boundaries for that world. At school—even at day care—children learn very quickly that the teacher is in charge of them and the classroom, but that the principal oversees the entire school and is the ultimate authority figure. If you're putting me in charge—as the teacher—you, as the principal, have to be the one to explain the rules so she knows that you back me up and that she'll be sent to the principal's office if she doesn't behave appropriately toward the teacher."

"Fine. I can take care of that right now."

Annalise shook her head. "There are too many distractions here. It's better to do it in the setting where we're going to spend most of our time."

"I have a full schedule today."

Her mouth took on a stubborn slant. "No, right now you have a family obligation that takes precedence over your full schedule."

"Damn it." He allowed himself an entire ten seconds to stew. "You're right, of course. I don't like that you're right. But, Isabella comes first."

She didn't attempt to disguise her relief. "You have no idea how happy I am to hear you say that."

"Go pack her up. Tell the sitter he can leave. I'm sure he'll be only too happy to run for the nearest exit." He lifted an eyebrow. "You sure you don't want to join him?"

Stark emotion shifted through her gaze, rousing his curiosity. For some reason his niece had made quite an impact on Annalise. He'd seen that look in others when they'd seized on a project or an idea that touched them in some way. In just the short time since he'd hired his new nanny, she'd bonded with Isabella and would do whatever necessary to make certain the relationship worked.

"I'm staying," she said quietly, confirming his conjecture.

For the first time Jack felt a stab of genuine hope. So far, so good. "Thank you, Annalise."

Once his PI had gone over her background and given the all clear, Jack would move his marriage project to the next stage. In the meantime, if Annalise became emotionally connected to Isabella, so much the better. It might make her more amenable to his proposal. All he had to do was find the right buttons to push to convince her to cooperate, something he hoped the investigation might assist in uncovering.

The ride to his home was accomplished in blissful silence. Isabella went into her booster seat without a word—or rather, sound—of complaint. He wished it signaled an improvement, but he suspected she was merely resting up for the next round.

Heading into the South of Broad neighborhood of Charleston, Jack turned onto Battery and hit the remote control for the electric gates. Beside him, Annalise reacted to her first glimpse of Lover's Folly with a soft gasp. "Home sweet home," he murmured. "Hope you like it."

Whatever facade she'd managed to don over the past few hours crumbled. "You live here? This is your home?"

Even he had to admit the four-story, nearly eleven-thousand-foot residence created quite an impact. Meticulously renovated over the past several decades, it boasted views of Charleston Harbor and James Island, and was listed as an exceptional example of historic architecture.

"It's called Lover's Folly, and I inherited it from my paternal grandmother, much to my father's annoyance. He assumed he was next in line to own the place. It's been in the family since the mid-nineteenth century, a decade or so before the War Between the States. My ancestors bought it from the original owner."

"Why is it called Lover's Folly?"

He pulled his Jaguar into the two-story brick carriage house, the structure large enough to house a half dozen vehicles, if he were given to that sort of excess. His housekeeper, Sara, shared the two bedroom apartment above the garage with her husband, Brett, who was employed as the gardener and general handyman.

"It was constructed as an apology to the man's wife—" He spared a quick glance toward the backseat. To his relief, Isabella was sound asleep, no doubt worn out from her morning exertions. He lowered his voice. "When his wife found out he'd been keeping a mistress in high style, she demanded recompense. He had this house built to make up for his folly."

A smile trembled on Annalise's mouth. "For his folly for taking a mistress or for getting caught?"

Jack grinned. "No one's quite certain, though there's been endless speculation about that." He exited the car and gently extracted Isabella from the backseat. She murmured groggily before burrowing against him and nodding off again. It was rare moments like this that convinced him he'd done the right thing, that this poor little mite needed him. "She's exhausted, which means she'll nap for a while. Enjoy it while it lasts."

"I gather it doesn't last long?"

"No."

That single, terse word said it all. He led the way into the kitchen and introduced Annalise to Sara. The housekeeper offered a warm smile before turning a wary eye on Isabella. "Little Madam is worn out, I see. But it must have gone well, considering you managed to hire another nanny."

Jack slanted Annalise a quick, encouraging look. "One who plans to stay, I hope." He inclined his head toward the steps at the far end of the kitchen. "I'll be up in the nursery if you need me."

He ascended the back staircase, climbing to the second floor. The nursery wing occupied the right-hand side of the U-shaped mansion. It had been designed in the days of large families and live-in servants, and consisted of four bedrooms, plus the nanny's quarters, and a huge playroom. He carried Isabella into the room she'd chosen for herself. It overlooked a large patio and yard, and was enclosed by a towering stone wall. After settling his niece in her bed, he picked up the baby monitor and hooked it to his belt. Then he motioned to Annalise and escorted her to the playroom, where they could talk without disturbing Isabella.

The instant they entered the room, Annalise spun around to face him. She did her best to hide it, but she was seriously rattled. A deep flush sculpted her sweeping cheekbones, while her eyes rivaled the sun in their intensity. Though she stood without moving, the ringlets which had escaped her control trembled in agitation.

She took a deep breath, drawing his attention downward to where the vee of her jacket clung to the attractive swell of her breasts and traced the outline of her narrow waist and the womanly flare of her hips. For some reason the nondescript black suit didn't seem so nondescript anymore. Not when he examined all it concealed.

His nanny was a knockout.

"Color me officially overwhelmed," she announced.

"I have every confidence that you'll acclimate," he replied.

Worry dug a small line between her brows.

"I'm not so sure. I've only seen the smallest fraction of this place and I'm already blown away."

"Relax, Ms. Stefano. One of the reasons I hired you was your impressive self-control."

"No, the reason you hired me was because all the other rats had deserted the sinking ship." She paced off a small measure of her agitation, giving him an excellent view of her endless legs and gloriously rounded backside. She spun around to face him. "Is this the sort of home Isabella came from?" she asked. "Was she accustomed to this sort of grandeur? To living among so many antiques?"

Jack forced himself to ignore the tantalizing view and focus on the business at hand. "No, Joanne and her husband, Paul, lived a far more simple life."

Annalise's expression grew troubled. "So many changes, poor baby," she murmured. "It must be even more overwhelming for her than it is for me."

"This is where and how I live. In time, my niece will become accustomed to it. She won't have any choice." He lifted an eyebrow. "Unless you expect me to sell a home that's been in my family for over a hundred and fifty years?"

She waved that aside. "No, of course not." She regarded him in momentary silence and he could see her marshaling and organizing her thoughts and impressions. "May I ask a personal question?"

Not a road he wanted to head down. Nonetheless, he inclined his head. "Feel free."

"How did you gain custody of Isabella? Did your sister request you as guardian in her will?"

"It would have simplified matters if she had. Unfortunately, she didn't."

"So, you simply took your niece in? There was no one else?"

Anger flashed through him. He planted his fists on his hips and faced her down. "You say that as though you don't consider me an appropriate guardian."

She hesitated. "That's not the word I'd use. You have a…a magnificent home. You're a successful businessman. You're well-intentioned—"

"But?"

She frowned. "Weren't there any other family members willing to take her? Someone who has more time to devote to her care?"

"No. Paul has a sister. She flat out refused."

"Flat out? But, why?"

"Because Isabella isn't blood kin. Joanne and Paul adopted Isabella when she was only a few days old. For some reason, that let Paul's sister off the hook."

"And put you on it?" Annalise had adopted an expressionless mask again. But he'd begun to realize that the less emotion she showed, the more she felt. "Is that why you took her in? Because no one else stepped up?"

He gave her the look that would have most men in his rarified world trembling in their Berluti loafers. "Ms. Stefano, I hired you as Isabella's nanny, not as my personal pop psychologist. My reasons for assuming guardianship of Isabella have nothing to do with you or the job you are to perform. A job for which I'm paying you quite a lot of money."

To his amazement, she didn't back down. In fact, she took a step closer. "Have I hit a hot button, Mr. Mason? Did you feel obligated to take her in? Are you protecting your image? Concerned with media scrutiny? Is that why Isabella's here, so your personal and business image don't take a hit?"

Fury vied with a primal awareness, one with a raw, sexual edge. Or perhaps the fury exacerbated the awareness he'd experienced the first moment he'd set eyes on her. "You are walking a very thin line, Ms. Stefano. If I had anyone who could take your place, I'd fire you on the spot."

"For asking tough questions? Or do my questions hit a little too close to home?"

Her questions were identical to those Mrs. Locke had asked. That alone gave him pause. He was a private man who kept his personal life as far from the high beams of the media headlights as possible. He also kept his emotions under tight control, even tighter than Annalise did. Another lesson he'd learned at his father's knee. As much as he hated the idea, he needed this woman. Isabella needed her. She might be the only person capable of keeping his tiny family intact.

He forced himself to answer her. "Other than Paul, Isabella was the most important person in my sister's life." He swallowed past the tightness constricting his words. "At one point, Joanne was the most important person in mine. Isabella is part of my sister, all that's left of her. My niece is hurting and I have no idea how to help her."

The anger drained out of Annalise. "You hired me to take care of Isabella. And that's what I intend to do." She gestured in the general direction of his niece's bedroom. "Tell me something, do you think that overstuffed toy factory you call a bedroom is in her best interest?"

What the hell was she talking about now? "It's

the smallest of the bedrooms. She chose it herself."

Annalise's breath escaped in a quiet sigh. "The issue isn't the square footage of her room. I couldn't even say what size it is because it's stuffed to the rafters with toys and games."

"I'm just trying to create a home for her."

"By buying her *things*. That's not how you create a home. Isabella doesn't need *things*. She needs love and attention."

"I'm doing the best I can." He hated the gritty quality that climbed into his voice.

Annalise took note and a softness slipped into her voice. "Your niece doesn't need more stimulation, Jack. She needs less."

For some reason, her use of his first name had a devastating effect. He forced himself to listen to Annalise's words, when what he really wanted to do was yank her closer and see if all that passion would spill over into their embrace. Would spill onto him. She gave so generously of herself to a little girl she didn't even know.

How would it feel to have some of that emotion directed at him?

The instant the thought blazed through his mind, he rejected it. Damn it to hell! Had he lost every ounce of common sense? This wasn't part of the plan.

He deliberately turned his back on Annalise and walked to the window, giving himself some much needed breathing room. Resting his arm on the sash, he gazed out at the backyard. It had been designed as a peaceful haven, secluded from the bustle and noise of the city traffic. He retreated there whenever he had a tough business decision to make—or a tough personal one. It was there that he'd made the final determination to accept responsibility for Isabella. It was there he'd come to the conclusion that he'd have to marry in order to retain custody of his niece. Would it be Annalise who ultimately became his wife?

He turned around, surprising a look of compassion on her face. "CPS wants to take Isabella away from me," he found himself admitting.

Annalise couldn't quite control her flicker of alarm. "Why? What did you—" She broke off abruptly. "What concerns them?"

"That's not what you were about to say." It was his turn to close the distance between them. "You were wondering what I'd done wrong that caused CPS to step in."

Her breathing quickened as she finally seemed to sense she'd pushed him too far. "Why are they involved?"

"I already told you. Paul and Joanne didn't designate a guardian. CPS needs to make sure I'll do an adequate job." His mouth twisted. "So far they're less than impressed."

"But you mean to change that."

He fixed her with a fierce look. "Allow me to make myself clear." He paused to give his words more impact. "I'll do whatever I must in order to keep Isabella. Any. Damn. Thing. Is that clear enough, Ms. Stefano?"

"Annalise."

Why didn't she back down? Did she know

nothing about his reputation? Or did she simply not care? "You're not the least intimidated by me, are you?"

She lifted an eyebrow. "Should I be?"

"Yes," he stated baldly. "But you're like a damned dog with a bone. You just don't let go."

She stunned him by leaning in and offering a teasing smile. "Isn't that precisely the sort of person you want on Isabella's side? I'm a fighter. And you're right. I don't give up."

He paused to consider. He did need someone like her, someone who'd help him take on Mrs. Locke. Maybe it was time to listen to her. "What do you suggest?"

She didn't hesitate. "Two things. First, simplify Isabella's environment so she isn't so visually stimulated and overwhelmed. Second, I suggest you take a few weeks off work and spend time with her in a—" she spared a brief glance around "—shall we say, in a more basic setting."

"I can't afford to take a few days off right now, let alone a few weeks."

Annalise tilted her head to one side, and more curls escaped from the knot at her nape, tumbling down her shoulders and back in glorious abandon. No wonder she attempted to maintain such tight control over her hair. It was every bit as willful as the rest of her. Her eyes darkened as she regarded him.

"I thought you were willing to do whatever it took to keep custody of Isabella," she said. "Any. Damn. Thing. Remember?"

"I have a business empire to run."

"Then let her go."

The softly spoken recommendation—identical to the one his lawyer, Derek, had made—hung in the air between them, vanquished only when he released a single, harsh expletive. "I must have been insane when I hired you."

"Would it help if I promise I'll always put Isabella's best interests first?"

"I don't doubt that for a minute." He forked his fingers through his hair. Every instinct told him she was right. He'd just been looking for an easier solution. He should have known he wouldn't find one. Building his import/export business had been no different. It had required total dedication and had demanded his attention every hour of every day, and then some. "Fine. We'll try it your way for now."

Her grin blew him away. "Thank you."

He snagged the collar of her suit jacket and tugged her close. Close enough that he could feel the explosion of her breath against his jawline. "We'll try it your way for now. But one stumble and that changes. Are we clear, Ms. Stefano?"

"Are you a perfectionist, Mr. Mason? Are your employees expected to be just as perfect?"

She'd reverted to a more formal manner of addressing him and he could guess why. Since she couldn't pull free of his hold without losing their small battle of wills, this was her subtle way of putting some distance between them. "Jack," he reminded her. "And yes, I am a perfectionist. I can afford to be—just as I can afford to hire the very best and expect them to give me precisely what I want."

She didn't cave, not one inch. Instead, she continued to gaze at him with those ancient, deep-set eyes, eyes that seemed to alter color with her every mood change. Right now, they reminded him of tarnished gold. "In that case I'll have to see that you get your money's worth."

His gaze dropped to her mouth, a mouth full and lush and red, and more enticing than the legendary apple Eve had offered Adam. "I'll hold you to that," he warned.

Temptation beckoned, urging him to take a bite of sin. He didn't bother resisting. Something about this woman made him want to stake his claim, to gather up all that passion and energy she tried so hard to hide and allow it to storm through him. He'd been so cold for so long. He needed her heat, needed to feel the flames of desire. To—just this once—release the rigid control which governed every aspect of his life. What harm would this one time make?

Was she as curious as he to see where their embrace took them? He could spare her the suspense. He'd accomplished step one of his marriage project. He'd hired a nanny who would put his niece's best interests first and stick around long enough to satisfy CPS. Now for step two. To engage her emotions just enough that she'd cave to the insanity of marrying him.

He lowered his head and captured her mouth with his. He half expected Annalise to yank free of the embrace, but to his relief, she didn't resist. Nor did she burn with the same fire sweeping through him. Instead, she responded with a heady delicacy. Her mouth turned soft and responsive, yielding for those first seconds. Then her lips parted ever so cautiously, and she deepened the kiss.

Rational thought disintegrated. All he could think about was the woman in his arms and how quickly he could strip away the layers of clothing until burning flesh collided with burning flesh. He skated his hands down her back and cupped her lush backside, pulling her more fully against him. His groan slid from his mouth to hers.

A soft moan hummed in her throat and she slid her hands across his chest to his shoulders. "Jack…"

The sound of his name, overflowing with feminine desire, swept away the final remnants of his self-control. He urged her backward across the room toward the padded window seat overlooking his cloistered garden. The back of her legs bumped against the half-wall and she teetered on the edge of tumbling. He grinned against her mouth, preparing to follow her down onto the thick cushions, when an unmistakable noise distracted him. The sound of weeping crackled through the baby monitor clipped to his belt.

He released Annalise, and for an endless second their gazes locked and held. Shock and disbelief glittered in her eyes, though whether directed at his actions or her own, he couldn't quite tell.

The breath exploded from her lungs and she shook her head. "Oh, no. *Hell,* no. This is not going to happen ever again, Mr. Mason. Are we clear on that point?"

"Crystal. And just so you know?" He traced a finger along the curve of her cheek and watched as her eyes overflowed with helpless desire. She fought it, but it was there for him to see. "It will happen again, for one reason and one reason only."

Her chin shot up. "And what's that?"

"I doubt either of us will be able to keep our hands off each other."

With that, he turned and left the room, unwilling to admit even to himself how difficult he found the choice.

Three

Isabella crouched in the middle of the large bed, lost amid the piles of pillows, dolls and stuffed animals. He crossed to sit on the edge of the bed. Annalise appeared in the doorway behind him and stepped hesitantly into the room.

"Hey, Baby Belle," he murmured. It had been his sister's nickname for her daughter and using it often helped soothe Isabella. "All done with your nap?"

She stared up at him, her green eyes dewy wet and far too resigned for a child of five. She nodded in response to his question before turning her attention to Annalise. To Jack's surprise his niece didn't scream as she often did with the other nannies he'd hired. Nor did she appear the least interested. Instead, she stared with apathetic acceptance. He sighed. Too many changes in too short a period of time.

"Isabella, this is Annalise. She's your new nanny. The three of us are going to spend the day together getting to know each other."

Recalling Annalise's concern about the room, Jack swept a swift assessing glance around. Now that he looked—really looked—the place resembled nothing more than a toy store that had exploded in messy exuberance. She was right. The kaleidoscope of colors created an agitated blur that didn't allow the eye to settle. Why the hell hadn't he noticed it before?

"You know—" he offered tentatively "—it's pretty crowded in here, isn't it? There's hardly any room for you, let alone all these toys. I wonder if your new nanny can fix that problem."

No response from his niece, but Annalise caught the ball he lobbed in her direction and put it in play. "You're right, Jack. It is too crowded in here." She took a seat on the floor, folding her lanky frame so her height wouldn't seem as intimidating. "I'll bet your toys would like to have their own room so they're not so uncomfortable crammed in here. What do you think, Isabella? Shall we pick out a special room where your dolls can stay when you're not playing with them?"

A debate raged in vivid detail across Isabella's face. She shot Jack a questioning glance. At his smile of encouragement, she nodded in agreement.

"Why don't you pick out your favorite dolls and put them on the bed," Annalise suggested, pitching her voice so it remained calm and non-threatening. "They'll stay here with you. Then we'll pick out a special room for the others."

Isabella hopped off the mattress and made a beeline across the room. She seized a porcelain doll that had seen better days and placed it with great care on the bed. To Jack's amazement, she turned and faced Annalise, waiting for the next instructions.

"That's the only one?" he prompted. He couldn't explain why he was so horrified when she nodded. "If you want another—"

Annalise shook her head in silent warning. "What about the stuffed animals?" she asked. "Are there any who should stay with your doll?"

This time Isabella gathered up three: a thread-bare puppy, a cashmere-soft kitten and a ferocious lion. Over the next half hour, Annalise worked her way through each type of toy until the favorites had been whittled down to a select couple dozen.

When she'd finished, Jack found he had to swallow hard before speaking. "They're all the toys she brought from home," he commented in a rough undertone. "She's spent three full months here with hundreds of brand-new toys and all she wants—"

To his horror, he couldn't finish his comment. Fresh grief welled up inside, ripping through him. What was money in comparison to Joanne and Paul? What were all these toys he'd drenched his niece in, compared to the lives of her mother and father? He'd trade every penny of his billions to have his sister and her husband alive and well. But that wasn't possible. And so Isabella clung to the tattered remains of that old life while he clung to Isabella.

Beside him, Annalise gathered his hand in hers and squeezed gently. She waited until he'd regained his self-control before continuing. "Anything you've forgotten about?" she asked Isabella.

There was a momentary hesitation and then she darted to the small bedside table and snatched up a picture frame, hugging it close. It was too much. Jack was at Isabella's side in an instant, lifting her into his arms. He took a seat on her bed and cradling her close. "Don't worry about your pictures," he murmured. "They all stay in here. Every last one of them."

Gently he pried the frame from her grasp so they could both study the photo. Joanne and Paul beamed out at them, a slightly younger version of Isabella tucked protectively between the two. He ran his index finger over his sister's image. Memories crashed over him like waves advancing before a storm front.

"Your mom and I looked alike, didn't we?" he managed to ask his niece. Not that he expected a response. To his surprise, she leaned her slight weight against him and nodded.

His sister's rich, brown hair was a couple shades lighter than his, the highlights more red than the gold that streaked his own hair. But they shared the same facial features—straight, bold noses, full mouths, squared jawlines. Even the direct intensity of Jo's black eyes was identical to what he saw reflected in his mirror each day. These were characteristics they'd inherited from their mother, something that connected the three of them.

"God, I miss her," he said. Isabella curled tighter into his embrace and he could feel her shoulders tremble, feel the dampness of tears soaking into his shirt. He wrapped her up close and planted a kiss in her matted curls. "We'll get through this, Baby Belle. I swear we will. You and I are going to be a family. It won't be the same as it was. But we'll figure it out. Somehow we'll manage."

He didn't know how long they clung to each other. Throughout it all, Annalise remained quiet and motionless, giving them the time they needed to weather the storm. When the last hiccupped sob had long faded, Jack drew Isabella to her feet. His hand swallowed hers as he led her to the bedside table. Carefully, he returned the photo to its place of honor.

He crouched beside her. "They'll always be watching out for you, Isabella. Just like I will. Okay?"

Isabella nodded solemnly. Then Annalise crossed to join them. "Why don't we go find that special room for the rest of your toys?" The gentle suggestion came at the perfect moment, helping to distract them from their sorrow. "Anytime you want one of the toys from that room, you can trade them. That means you pick one of the toys from in here and put it in the special room and take the toy you'd like to play with instead and bring it in here to live with you. Is that all right?"

Isabella sought Jack's reassurance before nodding. Over the next hour, they made a production of choosing the perfect "special room" and transferring toys. When they were done, his niece's room had been transformed from a toy store into a peaceful, uncluttered bedroom. Her favorite toys decorated the shelves lining her room, each assigned a place of honor. He noticed that all the books remained, as well as a small play station that contained puzzles, coloring books and other educational toys.

"Makes quite a difference, doesn't it?"

Annalise murmured. "This gives her a safe haven that should help her relax."

"Instead of a place guaranteed to agitate."

He glanced at her, driven to mention what had happened in the playroom. Before he could, she spoke again. "Did the caseworker see Isabella's room with all the toys?"

He grimaced. "Yes."

To his surprise she rested a hand on his arm and gave a reassuring squeeze. "Don't worry. I'm sure it will help once she sees the changes you've made."

It was the second time they'd touched since their embrace in the playroom. Not that she seemed aware of that fact. He wound one of her curls around his finger and tugged. "The changes *you're* making, don't you mean?"

She stilled and her pulse fluttered at the base of her neck. Standing this close he could see the smooth, rich texture of her skin, the color a gorgeous creamy shade accentuated by her dark hair. The attraction he felt drew him, even as he fought to hold himself at a distance. He shouldn't be experiencing these emotions. They weren't part of the plan. And yet, they were undeniable. What the hell would happen once they eventually married?

If they married, he hastened to correct himself. He had a long path to walk from here to the altar. Considering Annalise's willful nature, it wouldn't be an easy one.

As though underscoring that point, she eased free of his touch and focused her attention where it belonged...on Isabella. "I couldn't have made any changes if you weren't here to reassure your niece and lend support." She shot him a warning look. "Nor will I be able to make any more if we're not in agreement on how our...relationship should progress from here."

He had to give the woman credit. Subtle, yet direct. Too bad she hadn't chosen to enter the business world. She'd have been a natural. "So, what's next on the agenda?" he asked with a calm he didn't come close to experiencing.

"Lunch, I hope." A swift smile flashed. "Dare I suggest something casual, either al fresco or in the kitchen?"

"We'll eat on the patio. Sara's not too keen on having her kitchen invaded," he explained.

The choice proved a rousing success. The serene location had a beneficial effect on Isabella. After they arranged for a place setting for her doll, she ate without protest or tears, and afterward played beneath a nearby tree, rocking her "baby" while humming tuneless reassurances.

"It won't last," Annalise offered. She dipped a hand in a glass bowl containing a selection of olives and popped one in her mouth. "I just want to warn you so you don't get your hopes up."

"And here I was assuming you had waved your magical wand and fixed all our problems."

She cocked an eyebrow. "Sorry. The fairy godmother association hasn't issued me my official wand yet. Until they do, we'll have to handle this the old-fashioned way."

"Hard work and luck?" he guessed.

"Mmm. We *were* lucky today. Tomorrow…?" She shrugged. "Who knows? I do have another suggestion, however."

"Go on."

"If there's any way you can arrange it, we should institute step two as soon as possible. Can you take a couple weeks off sometime in the near future?"

"And go where?" A hint of cynicism crept into his voice. "The Caribbean? Hawaii? Europe?"

"Is that what you think I'm after? A free vacation?" Laughter brightened her eyes. "No way, ace. I'm talking low-key. A little bungalow on one of the islands around here. Someplace modest where the three of us are tripping all over each other so we're forced to bond."

"Dangerous, all that bonding."

Color dotted her cheeks and he could see the reflection of those moments in the playroom mirrored in her eyes. "Focus, Mason. I'm talking about bonding with Isabella," she stated tartly.

"Once we've spent some quality time together, we can come back here. It would help if you could transition to working part-time and hang around here with your niece the rest of the day."

"Hell, honey. If I do all that, what am I paying you for?"

Annalise didn't take offense, though her chin jerked upward an inch in open challenge. "You're paying me to help Isabella adjust to a brand-new life, a life she didn't expect or want or ask for. You're paying me to get CPS off your back, although you neglected to mention that small detail during our interview."

"Sorry." He scrubbed his hands across his face. "You're right, of course. I'm not handling this well. Blame it on exhaustion."

It took her a minute to work out the reason. "Isabella's nightmares?"

He nodded. "It's hard to get her settled afterward. I'm down to about five hours a night. She can sleep during the day to make up for it, but I can't."

"That explains a lot. Isn't there someone who can cover for you at night? What about the woman you mentioned during the interview?" She fumbled for a name. "Mrs. Walters?"

"She's here five to ten but refuses to live in. And I've had enough trouble finding someone for the day shift without running the risk of losing Walters. I need her for those occasions I work late or have a meeting out of town. Besides, the nights I'm with Isabella..." His mouth compressed. "You've talked about my bonding with my niece. Well, the nights when I sit with her, comforting her while she drifts back off to sleep, those are the times we come closest to bonding."

Annalise nodded in perfect understanding. "And you don't want to give them up."

"No." His response caused a hint of relief to flicker across her face. His back teeth clenched. "My guardianship of Isabella isn't just about duty, Ms. Stefano, despite what you clearly believe."

A smile quivered at the corners of her mouth. "Do you realize that whenever you're annoyed with me, you revert to formality?"

"Take it as a warning."

Annalise's smile grew and Jack stared in disbelief. Why didn't she react the way every other intelligent person within his sphere of influence did when confronted with the predatory side of his nature? She should be quaking in her sensible flats. She should be utterly intimidated by the slightest frown. Hell, she should be doing precisely what he said without a single word of argument. Instead, she helped herself to another olive and popped it in her mouth as though lounging across from a man capable of destroying her world was an everyday occurrence.

"Do you have no sense of self-preservation?" he demanded.

She blinked, mildly startled. "Excuse me?"

"You are familiar with my name, I assume? With my reputation?"

She frowned. "Sure. Who isn't?"

"What, may I ask, do you know about me?"

She shrugged. "You're thirty. You're rich. Powerful. You were supposed to go into the family business with your father. Instead you walked away. When you were cut off from the Mason purse strings, you built an import/export empire from scratch that succeeded in eclipsing your father's in the business world. You've been linked, romantically, with some of the most beautiful women in the world." She blinked at him in open bewilderment. "Is it important that I know your history? Will it help somehow with Isabella?"

He gritted his teeth. "No, but it should help in *our* dealings."

Her eyes narrowed, then widened. Her mouth gave another betraying quiver before she bit down on her lip to suppress it. "I'm so sorry, Mr. Mason. Have I neglected to treat you appropriately?"

"Instant obedience to my every whim would be appreciated," he responded dryly.

A gurgle of laughter escaped. She leaned

forward and pitched her voice to an ingratiating purr. "Very well, sir. Your every wish is my command, no matter how boring and tedious all that instant gratification may become."

He fought for a control that should have come without thought or effort. But ever since Annalise had entered his life with her distinctive hip-swinging stride, that control had eluded him. He couldn't help himself. He released a barking laugh, unable to recall the last time he'd felt such genuine amusement. Isabella's head jerked up and she stared at him in open disbelief, as though the sound was not only unheard of, but downright impossible. Sorrow caused his humor to fade. Was his laughter really such a rare occurrence?

Annalise followed the progression of his thoughts with uncomfortable accuracy. "Okay, I get it. You're a ruthless businessman. But who are you to Isabella? How do you want her to respond to you, Jack? Should she fear you, or should she look on you as her kind and loving uncle?"

He shook his head. "It's not like I have a choice. I am what I am."

"Are you saying you're incapable of kindness? Of love?"

He turned his gaze on her, one he didn't doubt reflected the wintry coldness that seized hold. "Those qualities were eradicated long ago. What I can give my niece is a home, financial security and as much attention as I can spare."

"Got it. That sounds a lot like duty and obligation to me. And yet, not two minutes ago you claimed that wasn't why you took Isabella in. You might want to consider which is most accurate." She fixed him with an unwavering stare. "And I suggest you choose one that CPS will buy."

"You want me to lie?"

"Right now, I'm not sure even you know what's truth and what's lie."

He swore beneath his breath and surged to his feet. He'd had enough of this touchy-feely stuff. Time to take control, and this time he wouldn't let

Annalise wrest it away again. "I think we need to discuss what happened earlier in the playroom."

His comment struck a nerve. She deliberately turned her head in Isabella's direction. His niece remained fully engaged with her doll. "I believe I already addressed that issue. It won't happen again."

"Time will tell."

She followed his example and thrust back her chair. He couldn't begin to imagine the amount of inner fortitude it took for her to stand and face him. But somehow she did it. "I have no excuse for what took place earlier. I will tell you I'm no stereotype, despite that unfortunate incident. You're paying me to take care of your niece, not be your mistress. Decide now, Mr. Mason. Which do you want? A nanny or a mistress?"

"And if both roads end up in the same place?"

"I'll quit before I become your mistress. Is that clear enough?"

"Quite." He leaned his shoulder against one

of the beams supporting the wooden canopy that shaded the patio and folded his arms across his chest. "There's only one small problem."

"Which is?"

Her poise wasn't as secure as she'd like to pretend. He'd always been excellent at reading people and Annalise proved no exception. He caught the slightest quaver of her voice and the helpless balling of her hands. Even more telling, the pulse in her throat fluttered like a moth struggling to throw itself into the flames. And like that moth, she was irresistibly drawn to something guaranteed to deliver her into the arms of certain disaster.

His arms.

"I have a strict policy forbidding interoffice fraternization."

"I don't work in your office." The instant the words escaped, she inhaled sharply, aware of how much she'd given away with that single thoughtless comment. "I mean—"

He cut her off without compunction. "That

policy extends to all my employees. I've never treated anyone who works for me with anything other than complete and utter professionalism." He paused deliberately. "Until today. Until you. Why is that, do you suppose?"

Her eyes darkened and she shook her head in open denial. "I have no idea."

"Yes, you do." He hadn't budged an inch, and yet for the first time since they'd met, she took a step backward. "Something unexpected happened between us. Something that caused me to ignore one of my cardinal rules. Do you have any idea how unusual that is?"

"If CPS suspected we were involved, it would cause untold problems," she was quick to say. "You can't afford to risk that, not if you're sincere about keeping custody of your niece."

"I'm dead serious."

"Then her needs must come first."

"I agree. But that doesn't change what happened today." He straightened and took a step in her direction. "Nor does it change what's occurring between us right now. If our reaction to one another is this bad after one day, what will it be like after a week…a month…a year?"

"Stop it, Jack." He could see she wanted to continue her retreat, wanted it with an intensity that flowed off her in hot, desperate waves. A painful vulnerability settled over her, one that affected him more profoundly than he thought possible. She held up her hand to halt his forward progress. "Are you trying to convince me to quit? If that's your goal, you're succeeding."

He shook his head. "I don't want you to quit. But I'm not going to pretend that the attraction between us doesn't exist. In order to make our relationship work, we have to deal with what we're experiencing and decide how to handle it."

"Fine. That's easy enough." She sucked in a quick breath while scrambling to take charge of the situation. Not that he'd let her. "We ignore it. We are careful to never be alone together. And we absolutely, positively keep our hands off each other."

"My hands were only a small portion of the problem."

Her gaze flashed to his mouth. "Hands. Arms. Lips. And every other part of your body."

He continued toward her, booting her chair out of his path. It skittered across the flagstones with a squeak of surrender. "That's one option, I suppose."

"Oh, God," she whispered. "Please, Jack. It's the only option. If we can't control ourselves, I'll quit. I won't have any other choice. I can't lose control. I can't. Not ever again." She ground into silence as he halted a mere foot away.

Curiosity consumed him. "What happens when you lose control?" he asked softly.

To his concern, her chin quivered. "Nothing good."

"A lesson hard learned?"

"Exactly."

"Then I won't touch you first."

Jack hated making the promise. He was a

ruthless man. A man who let nothing stand between himself and his goals. A man who'd learned the hard way to give no quarter. But a single anguished look from a pair of tumultuous golden eyes had him relenting. Softening. Clearly, he'd lost his mind.

Annalise's relief was palpable. "Thank you, Mr. Mason," she said formally.

He turned from her, furious with himself for not taking advantage of what he'd been able to accomplish so far. Time was still of the essence. He needed to move her from the role of nanny to the role of wife as soon as possible. Even so, he couldn't bring himself to hurt her in the process.

"No problem." He glanced over his shoulder, forcing out a teasing smile. "If you change your mind, feel free to say something."

Her mouth relaxed into a shadow of her old grin. "You'll be the first to know, I promise."

His cell phone vibrated and he checked the caller ID. "It's my lawyer," he explained to

Annalise before distancing himself from her and taking the call. "What's gone wrong now?"

"Aren't we in a glass-half-empty mood."

"Do I have reason to be?"

"Only if you haven't found someone," Derek admitted.

"I found someone." He spared Annalise a brief glance. She'd joined Isabella beneath the tree, sitting close enough to participate in his niece's play, without invading the little girl's territory. "The trick will be keeping her. I may have pushed too hard, too soon."

"That's not like you."

"There's a reason for that," Jack responded wryly. Like having difficulty keeping his hands off her. "What's wrong now?"

"Actually, it's mixed news. I managed to postpone Mrs. Locke's next visit. Told her you and the new nanny and Isabella were all going off on a little trip together so you could bond."

Bond. The word continued to haunt him and had him clamping his back teeth together. "I thought you said the news was mixed. That sounds like good news to me."

"It would be if Locke hadn't also informed me that she plans to make a final report after her next visit."

"*What?*"

"Calm down, Jack. I'm going to fight it and I'm pretty certain I'll be able to delay things again. But it would help if you had a loving wife cum nanny in tow the next time the Locke woman comes calling."

"I'm working on it."

"Work harder. Does this one have the qualifications I suggested?"

"Yes. Not a lot of experience, but she does have the appropriate educational background."

There was a delicate pause, then Derek asked, "What's she like?"

Jack's focus strayed in Annalise's direction again. "Different," he stated succinctly.

"Good different?"

"Let's just say that our marriage won't be

dull." A sudden thought occurred to him. "Before I forget, I need you to contact our private investigator and have her thoroughly checked out. I know he did a preliminary run on all the applicants. Tell him to dig deeper on Annalise Stefano. I don't want any surprises that might come back to bite us."

"I'm on it. So, where are you going for your vacation?"

The question caught Jack off guard. "Come again?"

"I told Locke you were going away. That wasn't just hot air. You're going to have to actually do it."

"I can't afford the time right now." He felt like a broken record.

"Find a way." Before Jack could argue, Derek added, "What the hell do you think will happen if Locke discovers you've been going into work? She won't be happy."

"Damn it, Derek."

"It's either that or you take my earlier suggestion. Let Isabella go. You can find a good home for her. Then you can give your business all of your attention. You don't have to marry. You don't have to deal with CPS. No more headaches. No more stress."

No more Isabella.

Jack closed his eyes. "Enough. I'll do it."

"Have a nice vacation."

Jack snarled a final comment before flipping his phone closed and crossing the yard in long, ground-eating strides. Annalise and Isabella peered up at him with identical looks of curiosity.

"Good news," he announced. "Pack your bags. The three of us are going on vacation."

Four

Bright and early the next morning, Jack had all the luggage loaded and Isabella and Annalise installed in the car. She turned to him as they pulled down the driveway and smiled brightly.

"So, where are we going?" she asked.

He eased into the boulevard traffic before sparing her a brief glance. "You'll be pleased to know that I took your advice. I've arranged for us to stay at a small bungalow on the beach."

He was careful not to use the word *vacation*. When he'd said it the previous day, Isabella had reacted with something approaching hysteria. It wasn't until Annalise made the connection between the word and the accident that had claimed the lives of Joanne and Paul that she'd been able to figure out a way to comfort his niece.

Annalise grinned. "A bungalow on the beach, huh? Sounds fantastic."

"It's not quite as modest as you requested," Jack warned. "But I think it'll do."

"I'm sure it'll be perfect."

Her quiet confidence in his abilities affected him more than he cared to admit. He was thirty years old with a first-class education. He came from one of the oldest families in all of Charleston. He owned and operated a billion-dollar international company with countless employees at his beck and call, most of whom were confident in his overall abilities. But for some reason, he responded to Annalise's admiration like a cat being presented a bowl of cream. If he wasn't careful, he'd start purring.

"Part of the problem is that I need someplace that will allow me Internet access so I can stay in touch with the office."

"Of course," she agreed. "Perfectly under-standable."

"And a location that protects our privacy."

"An unfortunate aspect of your position in life."

"Luckily, I have a friend who owns an estate with a guesthouse right on the water. He's in Europe for the summer, so we're welcome to stay for as long as we want. It's only two bedrooms, but it has a kitchen." A sudden thought struck. "Do you cook?"

"Yes."

"Okay, now for the important question. Are you willing to? I realize it's not part of your duties, but I'd be happy to compensate you for the additional work."

"That's not necessary." Annalise turned her head to stare out the window. "I'm happy to help out."

"And yet, you sound annoyed." A sudden thought struck, one he could scarcely credit. "Have I offended you by offering to pay you extra?" he asked.

Annalise released a sigh and shifted in her seat to face him again. "Yes. The ridiculous part is, I can't figure out why."

Maybe not, but he could. "It's because of what happened yesterday. In the playroom," he clarified.

She stiffened. "You mean when we—" She broke off and spared Isabella a quick look. "You know."

"Yes, I mean when we *you know.* The 'you knowing' blended business with personal."

"Then I suggest we unblend them since there won't be any more of either 'you,' let alone 'know,' ever again."

He shrugged. "We can try, though I doubt we'll succeed. How do you take the color green and turn it back into blue and yellow? We can say we're going to keep all the colors separate, that we'll resist the temptation to…er…blend. But I can't even offer to compensate you for the extra duties you'll be taking on these next couple weeks without it offending you."

"I'll get over it, just as I'll get over the urge to do anymore blending."

"Be sure to tell me how that works for you. I'm afraid I'm still a vivid shade of green."

An attractive blush tinted her cheeks. She deliberately twisted around and engaged in a one-sided conversation with Isabella. He didn't push. There'd be plenty of time over the next couple of weeks to tempt her with more blending. Even if he couldn't engage her on a personal level, he hoped she'd become so attached to Isabella that she'd be willing to accept his proposal for his niece's sake. He just needed to find the right lever that would tip the scales in his favor.

He ignored the small prick of conscience that prodded him for his cold-blooded plan. He couldn't afford a conscience, not if he wanted to keep custody of Isabella. If his father had taught him nothing else in life, Jonathan Mason had proved himself an expert instructor on how to pursue one's goals with ruthless disregard. Nothing mattered but the end results. Not compassion. Not kindness. Not any of the gentler emotions.

Jack had been brought up with a single motto: *No matter what it takes*. And that was how he would respond to his custody battle. When it came to Isabella, he would do whatever he had to, no matter what it took.

He pulled into a broad drive, guarded by a ten-foot-high stone wall and a high-tech electronic security gate. He keyed in the code Taye had given him and, once the wrought-iron doors swung open, drove toward a mansion even more elaborate than his own. Beside him, Annalise's jaw dropped. He turned down a narrow, graveled pathway, just wide enough for his Jag, and followed it for several hundred yards to a bungalow snuggled between beach and marsh.

Beside him, Annalise relaxed, possibly because the bungalow was an exercise in simplicity in comparison to the main house. "It's lovely," she said with all sincerity.

He smiled in satisfaction. "I hoped you'd approve." He thrust his door open. "Come on. Let's check it out."

Even Isabella lost her more typical apathetic mien and showed some enthusiasm. She darted into the bungalow behind him, one arm wrapped around her doll, the other around her stuffed lion. Jack couldn't help but wonder if the lion was meant as a protector—not that he'd blame her if that were the case. If it added to her sense of security, he'd surround her with a dozen lions.

The front door opened onto a small foyer, which accessed the main living area and a small dining room that he could use as a temporary office. On the far side of the dining room was a snug kitchen. A hallway branched off the living room and he led the parade in that direction, fairly certain they'd find the bedrooms.

Jack opened the first door and a small, rusty "ooh" emanated from behind him. His heart skipped a beat at the sound and he felt a surge of hope. Maybe Annalise was right. Maybe this vacation *would* turn Isabella around. Maybe it would even get her talking again. He forced himself to stroll casually into the bedroom, not wanting to betray any sort of reaction to that almost-word, afraid it might alarm her.

Isabella followed him in and made a beeline for a huge wooden structure that was part bunk beds and part tree fort. She vanished into one portion of the fort, climbed through trap doors and along secret tunnels, ending up in a bed cradled in the branches of the manufactured "tree," complete with fabric leaves and stuffed animals hidden in various nooks and crannies. Her vivid green eyes glowed with happiness and Jack realized that nothing had ever given him greater pleasure than the sight of his niece's beaming face.

"Like it?" he asked, striving to keep all trace of emotion from his voice. She nodded eagerly and her blondish-brown ringlets bobbed around her flushed cheeks. "It's good to see her hair growing out," he murmured to Annalise, who came to stand beside him.

"Did they cut it off after the accident?"

He nodded. "According to the pictures I've seen, she had beautiful long hair. But there were so many scalp lacerations, the doctors were forced to cut away large chunks of it. It seemed best to even it up and then let it grow out again. I just never realized how much work it would take to keep it from matting."

Annalise released a chuckle. "The hazards of curly hair, I'm afraid. I can't tell you how many times I've been tempted to go for one of those super-short hairstyles Isabella's sporting."

He studied her bone structure for a long moment. "You'd look good no matter how you wore it."

"Thanks." She actually blushed. "The nice thing is, it'll give me something in common with Isabella. We can do our hair together."

He gave a short laugh. "Good luck. That was one of the battles her former nannies fought on a daily basis. She doesn't like anyone touching her hair."

"Probably because right after the accident it hurt her scalp. That shouldn't be a problem any longer." She spoke with a confidence he hoped would pan out, though he had serious doubts. "I'll work with her on it."

Jack examined the room with a frown. "I didn't realize there would only be children's beds in here. There's no way you'll fit in that tree fort."

She shrugged. "No big deal. I'll sleep on the couch in the living room."

"Let's check out the other bedroom before we decide."

She lifted an eyebrow. "*Your* room? I don't think so."

"Relax. I just thought if it had two beds we could move one of them in here."

Her mouth tilted into a smile. "You sure, Mr.

Mason? I could have sworn I saw a distinct green accent coloring that suggestion."

"Not at all, Ms. Stefano. I'm perfectly satisfied with our current relationship." He left her to ponder that while he crossed the hallway to the second bedroom. A huge king bed dominated the room. Annalise came to a stumbling halt behind him. "Puts paid to that idea," he said.

"The couch it is," she agreed. She spared a quick glance at her watch. "We have a couple of hours until lunchtime. I think I'll check out the kitchen and see what supplies I'll need to pick up before then."

"I asked Taye's housekeeper to take care of stocking the shelves and refrigerator. If she overlooked anything you think we'll need, you can call up to the main house and she'll be happy to have it delivered."

"Taye?"

"Taye McClintock. He owns the McMansion we passed on our way here."

Her lips twitched. "And is McClintock a McDreamy, a McSteamy or a McWeeny?"

"McWeeny?" Jack chuckled. Taye had been one of his best friends in college and possessed the face of an angel and the mind of a computer, and was the only man Jack had ever met who could romance a woman into his bed in five minutes flat. "Oh, Taye's definitely a McWeeny, as I'll be sure to inform him the next time I see him."

She stared in horror. "You wouldn't."

"Not only would I, but I will."

A fierce debate raged across her face before she turned on her heel. "I think I'll unpack the car and get organized."

He caught her arm. "The organizing can wait. I'll unpack the car, while you wrestle Isabella into a bathing suit. Then we'll hit the beach before the rays get too intense."

The idea clearly appealed and she nodded. "Sold."

Twenty minutes later, they were out the door

and spreading their beach towels on the empty stretch of beach. To his intense interest, Annalise wore a modest two piece in an emerald green that brought out the gold highlights in her eyes. The bottoms were a pair of shorts that skimmed the tops of her thighs and showcased her mile-long legs. The top was equally modest, resembling a cropped tank that left her midriff bare.

If she thought he'd find it less appealing than something scantier, she'd underestimated him. If anything, the outfit teased his senses, whetting his appetite rather than satisfying it. The top fluttered in a flirtatious manner while the bottom clung lovingly to her pert backside and toned thighs. His body clenched and he forced his gaze away. If he was this randy on their first day of vacation, God help him get through the next two weeks.

"I'm going for a quick swim," he informed Annalise. "Will you keep an eye on Isabella?"

"Of course. That's why I'm here."

"For some reason, I'm having trouble remembering that," he muttered.

The ocean had warmed significantly over the past few weeks of warm, humid weather. He struck out through the gentle swells, working himself hard. By the time he climbed from the water, he'd regained some semblance of control. To his amusement, Annalise and Isabella were busy working on a sand castle. His niece looked up at his approach and waved him over with heartwarming eagerness. She put a plastic shovel in his hands and pointed at the moat they'd started to dig around the castle.

"You want me to help?"

Her broad grin and enthusiastic nod had him setting to the task with a will. Over the next hour they worked diligently, their efforts stymied by the turning tide. The waves crept closer and closer, overflowing the moat and splashing up the sides of the castle ramparts. Isabella shrieked in a combination of protest and laughter, first racing away from the waves then dashing back to prop up the collapsed towers.

Little by little, the sea won the battle. When the final tower toppled, melting into a mere lump of its former glory, Jack gathered up their towels, then scooped his niece into his arms and tossed her over his shoulder, reveling in her laughing squeals of protest. Not even her flailing sandy limbs could curb his pleasure in the changes these few short hours had wrought.

"Time for lunch, munchkin," he announced.

They took advantage of the outdoor shower, rinsing away the sand before entering through the laundry room off the kitchen. While Annalise and Isabella changed, he raided the refrigerator and put together a selection of sandwiches. Then he headed for the bathroom. By the time he returned, he found his niece dressed and seated at the table eating one of the sandwiches, her hair clinging to her head in tidy, damp ringlets.

"I didn't hear any screaming," he murmured to Annalise. "How did you pull that off?"

"I let her help me with mine and then we reversed the process. So far, so good."

"Thank you," he said simply.

He didn't know how else to express his gratitude, except... He hooked her chin with the knuckle of his index finger and started to brush her mouth with his when he suddenly realized what he was doing. He froze and their gazes clashed. Her eyes were wide and startled and her breath escaped her parted lips in a soft gasp.

"I'm sorry," he murmured, inches from her mouth. "I wasn't thinking. I just wanted to thank you."

Everything about her teased his senses—her sweet, sweet fragrance, her silken touch, those glorious eyes—making him want to draw her into his arms and consume her, body and soul.

"Do you thank all your nannies this way?" she demanded.

"Only you." His voice roughened. "I can't explain it."

"You promised not to touch me again."

He deliberately released her and took a step back, amazed at the strength of will it required. "Better?"

For a split second he thought she was about to say, "No." That she'd be the one to take that forbidden step into his arms and finish what he'd started. Then she nodded and deliberately turned away. The next instant acute tension tightened the muscles of her back and shoulders. A single look told him why.

Isabella had stopped eating and stared at them with unmistakable intensity. He couldn't tell whether their embrace had upset his niece or pleased her. Maybe she wasn't sure, either. After an endless moment she smiled, giving her seal of approval. A small dimple winked in her cheek. Until that moment, he didn't even realize she had a dimple, so rare were her smiles. That's what Annalise had managed to accomplish in just one short day.

Jack returned his niece's smile. Whether his

dear nanny knew it or not, his niece's smile had just sealed Annalise's fate.

The next several days flew by. Annalise proved to be right on several fronts. Getting away and devoting his full attention to Isabella made a noticeable difference. Of course, it didn't solve all her problems. There was still the occasional tantrum, but to his relief they were few and far between. It also helped that the two adults presented a united front, making it clear that such behavior wouldn't be tolerated.

To Jack, the most telling change came when his niece stopped painting her face in swirls of black, red and violent purple, but switched to more cheerful pastels that reflected her improved outlook on life. Not that the war paint lasted for more than an hour or two each day. Their twice-daily beach visits washed it away almost as soon as she applied it. On the fifth day, she forgot to wear it altogether, and that was when hope took hold.

Maybe, just maybe, there was a pathway out of the darkness.

Jack had to admit that his favorite times were in the evenings when the three of them curled up on the couch together and chose a DVD from the extensive selection stocked on the shelves surrounding the wide-screen TV. There in the darkness, he could relax his guard and simply enjoy this moment out of time.

"I think she's nodded off," Annalise whispered during one of their nightly sessions.

He'd sensed as much ten minutes ago when his niece's breathing had slowed and deepened and her muscles had gone lax against his chest. "I'll take her to bed in a minute."

"You like having her fall asleep on you, don't you?" The lights from the TV flickered, allowing him to catch the brief glitter of compassion reflected in her eyes. "Does it remind you of when you and Joanne were Isabella's age?"

Jack released a harsh laugh, one that had Isabella stirring in his arms. He traced a reassuring hand along his niece's back and forced himself to calmness. With a small, inarticulate murmur Isabella settled. "Not even close," he stated quietly. "My father would have considered this sort of activity a complete waste of time."

"Oh." That single word spoke volumes. "And your mother? Would she have also considered it a waste of time?"

He hoped the darkness concealed his expression, but he could hear the pain creep into his voice. "She was different than my father. Before their divorce she tried not to show her emotions, since he'd use any sign of weakness against her. She changed later on."

"How old were you when they broke up?"

"Eight. Nine, maybe. Joanne was two years older."

"And how did your mother change, afterward?"

"She softened, became more openly affectionate. Of course, it's hard to say if she was like that all the time. I can only base it on the time I saw her."

"What do you mean?" Annalise straightened, and he could feel her attempting to penetrate the darkness in order to read his expression. "Didn't your mother have custody of you?"

"No, only Joanne. My father took me."

He caught Annalise's soft gasp. "They split you up?"

"Yes." A wintry coldness settled over him. With that one single decision, every scrap of love and kindness had been removed from his life. He still felt the loss to this day. "My mother never spoke to me about that time, but Joanne once explained that our father threatened to take both of us and prevent our mother from ever seeing us again if she didn't agree to his terms."

A strobe of brilliance flashed across the screen, allowing him to see that Annalise was visibly shaken. "Could he have done that?"

"Considering I didn't see either my mother or

my sister again until I turned thirteen, I'd say not only could he, but he did precisely that."

"How…?" Her voice thickened, betraying her emotional reaction to his response. "Why…?" She shook her head, unable to formulate the questions she clearly wanted to ask.

Jack leaned his head back against the couch cushion and stared blindly at the old *Star Trek* movie that was Isabella's current favorite. "How? With some of the most powerful lawyers money could buy. Why? Because he was—and is—a total bastard who used me to hit out at my mother."

"But you did finally get to see her," Annalise said on a note of urgency.

A smile of satisfaction tugged at his mouth. "That I did."

"I assume he finally relented?" she asked tentatively.

"Not a chance in hell. The summer I turned thirteen, Dad took off overseas on an extended honeymoon with his latest trophy wife. I was supposed to go to camp. Instead, I hitchhiked to Colorado, where my mother was living with her second husband."

"Dear God, Jack!" She reached for him, her hand clutching his arm. "Do you have any idea how dangerous that was? Anything could have happened to you."

He regarded her with a hint of amusement. "That's what my mother said. It was worth it, though. I stayed with them for most of that summer." A summer filled with magic and hope. A summer unlike anything he'd experienced before or since. A summer that had ended in the death of dreams. "Until my father found out, that is. But those couple of months were quite eye-opening."

"In what way?"

His brows tugged together reflecting a hint of the bewilderment he'd experienced during that time period. "They were all so happy. They laughed almost all the time. And when they fought..." He struggled for the right words to explain. "I kept waiting for the other shoe to drop, but it never did."

"You mean when they fought, you weren't worried that they were on the verge of divorce." Her hand shifted, rubbing his arm in a soothing motion. He doubted she was even conscious of her actions. "They were never nasty toward each other."

"Exactly. They were—" he reflected on it for a moment "—casual. As though the way they interacted—the laughter, the tears, the squabbling, the open affection—was a normal, everyday occurrence."

"It probably was." She tilted her head to one side, sending a swath of curls tumbling across her shoulder. "How often did you get to visit after that?"

"I didn't. My disobedience that summer earned me a trip to military school. I didn't see Joanne again until I turned eighteen and my father no longer had any say in where I went or who I saw. Unfortunately, my mother and her husband managed to drive themselves off an icy mountainside a few months beforehand."

"Oh, Jack! How awful." He caught the betraying glitter of tears and felt something shift inside him, something deep and powerful. Something he wanted to protect himself from because it came from a wellspring of emotions he preferred to deny. "What happened to Joanne? Did she move back to Charleston to live with you and your father?"

"No. She was in college by then and flat out refused to have anything to do with our father."

"Or you?" she dared to ask.

He refused to acknowledge the hit. For years he'd believed just that, until Joanne had finally set him straight. But by then he'd found a way to insulate himself from the sort of emotional pain that came from sentiment and familial attachment.

"We managed to revive our relationship, despite my father." His mouth twisted. "Hell, Jo even found it in her heart to forgive him, not that he ever believed he required forgiveness. Ironically, Dad helped her find the lawyer who handled Isabella's adoption." Jack stood then, careful not to wake his niece, while putting an unmistakable period to the conversation. Annalise's hand fell away, leaving behind coldness where once there was warmth. "Time I put our little one to bed. I'll be back in a minute."

He took his time settling his niece, needing those handful of minutes to rebuild his barriers. He'd told Annalise far more than he'd shared with any other woman, opening parts of himself that he'd sealed away for almost two full decades. He didn't ordinarily let people in, didn't dare. That sort of closeness often became messy, risked creating emotions like the ones that had sent his parents' relationship spiraling into vicious arguments and acts of revenge.

He'd made up his mind at a very young age to avoid marriage at all costs. Even when he'd

witnessed firsthand his mother's loving relationship with her second husband, he still
hadn't trusted that their marriage was anything
other than pure dumb luck. The union he con-
templated with Annalise wouldn't involve an
emotional commitment. When they married it
would be carefully scripted with neat, tidy, legal
boundaries that specified every aspect of their
wedded "bliss" right down to the date of their
future divorce. As for any potential romantic en-
tanglements…

That would be determined by contract, as well.
He had no objection if she chose to share his bed.
But she would enter the affair with her eyes wide
open and all the cards on the table. He wouldn't
trick her with claims of affection. Theirs would
be a mating of body and intellect. A sensible
blending rather than an emotional one.

Satisfied that he'd fully regained his self-
control, he turned and found Annalise watching
him from the doorway. And that was when he

realized he had no self-control when it came to this woman.

None whatsoever.

Five

Jack had no memory of closing the door to Isabella's room. No memory of striding toward Annalise. No memory of backing her against the wall. But from the instant his mouth found hers, it was like a recorder flicked on, burning every tantalizing moment into the pathways of his brain.

He was overwhelmed by the distinctive fragrance of her skin and driven insane by the low, soft moan that reverberated in her throat. The heat of her hands and lips and flesh burned like wildfire, sweeping straight through to the frozen core of him and melting away walls of ice that he'd believed too tall and thick to ever be breached.

"I've tried, Annalise," he said between quick, biting kisses. "I've tried to keep my hands off you. How many times have I promised I would? And yet…"

A husky laugh exploded from her, and she leaned her head back against the wall, exposing her throat. "Somehow it doesn't quite work out that way."

"You don't understand. I always keep my word. Always. It's a point of honor with me. But with you—" Frustration tore through him. "It's like my body and brain are out of sync, or speaking different languages."

"No communication?"

"None." His hand drifted along the golden length of her neck. Then the urge to taste her consumed him and his mouth followed the same pathway his hand had taken. "Well, except for one single urge. On that point, all of the various parts of me are in total agreement."

A line from the movie they'd just watched played through his head: *Resistance is futile*. It described his predicament precisely. Temptation beckoned again and he fought it for all of ten seconds before he tumbled. Unable to help himself, he cupped her breast and traced the rigid peak through the thin cotton of her tank top. The breath exploded from her lungs and her sooty lashes fluttered toward her cheeks in clear surrender.

He used his knee to part her legs and settled into the cradle of her hips, sliding against a body that combined a lean, tensile strength with a sensual softness. He wanted her in his bed, wanted those endless legs wrapped around him. Wanted to sink into her warmth until the last vestige of ice had been driven from his body.

Everything about her propelled him toward a place he'd never been before, never even knew existed. A gentle place. A place of solace. A

place of beautiful urgency and endless pos-
sibilities. A place where he could safely lose
himself in arms that would never let him go,
while he basked in the warmth and light of her
embrace.

He reached beneath her tank top and found a
hint of what that sweet place would hold, and
he lingered there while the heat built. Her
breasts slipped into his hands, filling them with
their silken weight. Her nipples were two hot
buds of desire against his palms. He rocked his
hips into place between her legs, setting a slow,
torturous rhythm that ripped a moan from her
throat.

"Sleep with me tonight," he urged.

He watched the struggle play out across her
face, a fierce battle waged between common
sense and desire. He was intimately familiar with
that particular battle. For a brief instant he
thought she'd capitulate. But something held her
back, something that caused a glimmer of panic
to break across the planes of her face and an

intense vulnerability to tarnish her eyes. It would seem he wasn't the only one with painful memories.

"I can't. *We,*" she corrected, "we can't. Isabella has to come first. And if we do this, we'll be torn between responsibility and desire."

"I'll always put Isabella first."

"Then you won't fight me about this. Because having sex with you isn't putting Isabella first."

She didn't give him room to argue. Besides, she was right. They couldn't afford to be distracted right now. *He* couldn't afford it. He still needed her help. Somehow, someway, he had to find a way to convince Annalise to marry him. And that pathway led through her attachment to Isabella, not through his bedroom door.

As much as he wanted this woman, he couldn't have her. He reluctantly slid his hands from beneath her top and forced himself to abandon the warmth and softness he'd found for far too brief a time. He took a deliberate step backward. And then another. The want remained in her eyes, along with a hopeless res-ignation. If she'd uttered a single sound of regret, he'd have swept her into his arms and taken her then and there. But she remained silent. And he gave himself up to duty and re-sponsibility. The familiar cold returned, sweeping into his veins and taking root. How many years had it been his companion? He couldn't remember anymore. Not that it mat-tered. He'd learned long ago to accept the in-evitability of it.

Without a word, he turned and walked away.

Jack jerked awake at the sound of his bedroom door banging open.

"Is Isabella in here?" Annalise demanded. "Is she with you?"

He came off the bed like a shot. "She's missing?"

Annalise nodded rapidly, her breath escaping her lungs in frantic gasps. "When I went in to get her this morning she wasn't there. I thought she was hiding in the tree house. I practically took the thing apart looking for her. I've searched the entire house. She's not here." Undisguised fear glittered in her eyes, shredding her usual control. "I can't find her anywhere."

"Have you checked outside?"

"Oh, God, Jack." She turned a panicked gaze in the direction of the front door. "The ocean."

They both raced for the door. It wasn't locked and he could distinctly remember double-checking it last night to make certain it was. He ripped the door open and erupted onto the front porch. He drew in a deep breath, preparing to shout his niece's name, when suddenly he saw her. She sat halfway between the house and the water, half-buried beneath the largest dog Jack had ever seen.

Behind him, Annalise stumbled against his back. She inhaled sharply and he whipped around and caught hold of her. Sensing the scream building in her lungs, he covered her mouth with his hand.

"Quiet," he ordered in a voice barely above a whisper. "Don't startle them."

At her nod of understanding, he released her. "Jack," she whimpered. "That thing could kill her."

"Don't say it. Don't even think it. Right now, I want you to go back in the house and find my cell. Punch in 911, but don't hit Send until I tell you." She continued to stare at him with glazed, terror-stricken eyes and he gave her a quick shake. "Do you understand?"

She recovered a small semblance of control and nodded. "Yes. Yes, I understand. Dial 911. Don't hit Send until you give the word."

"Then I want you to grab the steaks that are in the fridge and bring them out here to me. Slow and easy, got it? No fast or sudden moves. No loud noises."

"I understand."

Without another word, she slipped back into the house. Jack forced himself to move forward and sit on the porch steps. Then he whistled, low and gentle. Both dog and child jerked to attention, their heads swiveling in unison toward him. To his horror, the dog bristled, emitting a low growl. Even worse, Isabella reached up to pat the animal on the muzzle, her tiny hand inches from a set of lethally bared teeth. He knew Annalise had returned by her soft gasp of reaction at how much more dangerous the situation had become.

"Here." She slipped the raw slabs of meat into his hand. Her fingers trembled against his and her breath warmed the back of his neck in rapid-fire bursts. She was inches from losing it, and yet she spoke with a calmness that washed over him like a gentle balm. "It's going to be all right, Jack. I have my hand on the Send button. Say the word, and I'll place the call."

"Go back inside," he instructed in an undertone. He wouldn't risk her welfare, too. "Be ready to open the door on my signal."

He sensed her silent retreat into the house and fixed his full attention on his niece and the huge animal hovering above her. He didn't dare whistle again. He could only hope that one or the other of them would come to him. Sure enough, Isabella released a gleeful laugh and clambered out from beneath the dog. To Jack's relief, the animal allowed it, though she—at least, he thought it was a female—continued to regard Jack with open suspicion bordering on hostility.

He needed to get the dog away from his niece, and fast. Hoping he wasn't making a hideous mistake, he held up the first steak. "Here you go, girl!"

It was as though someone had thrown a light switch. The hair along the dog's back slicked down and her ears perked up. A huge flirtatious grin spread across her giant square mug. After treating Isabella to a maternal lick of farewell from a tongue big enough to clean his niece's face with one swipe, she galloped toward Jack at top speed. Unfortunately, Isabella released a squeal of annoyance at having their play interrupted and gave chase. The instant the dog reached him, Jack tossed the first of the steaks. It disappeared in one less-than-feminine gulp.

"Sit," he ordered.

To his amazement, the dog sat. She checked him out—particularly the second steak he still held—while he did the same to her, a cautious how-beasty-are-you and who's-the-top-dog exchange of looks. She didn't appear to be in too bad a shape, though her ribs protruded more than he liked. After she'd given him the once-over, she regarded him with a look of unadul-terated hope and sweetness. To his relief, he saw that she wore a collar. He didn't see a name tag, but at least there was a shiny new rabies tag dangling from it.

His plan was to toss the second steak as far as he could, snatch up his niece and hightail it into the house. Before he could, Isabella skidded to a halt alongside the dog. He nearly lost it when she wound her twig-thin arms around the animal's massive neck and pressed her face into the short, brindled coat. One miscalculation and the dog would go from chewing on steak to chewing on his niece.

He forced himself to take a calming breath before speaking. "Isabella, go into the house and find Annalise. After you wash your hands, you can show her your new friend. You'll have to do it through the window until I've finished feeding her."

She hesitated, obviously torn between staying with the dog and the pleasure of showing her off to Annalise. He used a tone that didn't brook any argument, one he had never been able to bring himself to use with her. Until today. "Now, miss."

To his intense relief, she obeyed and climbed the steps onto the porch. The door flew open behind him and Annalise snatched her inside. With a whimper of protest, the dog charged forward and mowed all two hundred plus pounds right over top of him, snagging the steak out of his hands as she steamrolled past. Before Annalise could get the door closed, the dog slammed through it and erupted into the house.

Jack lay spread-eagled on his back, struggling just to draw air into his lungs. Getting hit by a Mack truck couldn't have been any more painful. He looked down at himself, half-expecting to discover paw craters denting his body. To his immense relief, he didn't find any. As far as he could tell, all his most vital parts appeared intact and in place.

He rolled over onto his hands and knees. It took three attempts to stand. He staggered through the door to find the dog squatting at Isabella's heels. Even sitting, the animal dwarfed the petite five-year-old, though there was no mistaking the adoration in the dog's brown eyes as she peered down at his niece. Isabella had her arms thrown around the animal's massive neck again. She beamed up at Jack with such undisguised joy it nearly broke his heart.

He closed his eyes with a groan. He knew

that look. "We're not keeping her," he stated categorically. "She belongs to somebody and that somebody isn't us."

To his surprise, Isabella didn't throw the expected temper tantrum. She just continued to stare at him with those dewy green eyes and that wide, brilliant grin. Her dimple gave a saucy wink.

"We don't know who owns her, Isabella," Annalise added. "The poor thing is probably lost."

"The 'poor thing' probably got dumped when she grew to the size of a baby elephant and started eating the owners out of house and home," Jack muttered.

It was precisely the wrong thing to say. Annalise turned on him with a horrified expression. "*Dumped?* You think she's been abandoned? Someone left her deliberately?"

Isabella tightened her arms around the dog who responded with a pathetic little whine that rattled every window in the bungalow. God help them if the beast ever cut loose with an actual bark. They'd end up with the roof caving in around their ears.

He spared his niece an uneasy look. "Then again, maybe someone is desperately trying to find her. I'll call Mrs. Westcott and find out if she knows anything about who the owners might be."

"Mrs. Westcott?" Annalise asked.

"Taye's housekeeper." Time to take control of the situation before this went any further. Jack fixed his niece with a steely gaze. "Give it up, sweetheart. We're not keeping the dog. She's wearing a rabies tag, which means she belongs to someone. I'm sure the owners are desperate to get her back."

Annalise intervened by resting a restraining hand on his arm. "She's a gorgeous animal," she commented in a blatant non sequitur. No doubt, it was her way of diffusing the standoff between uncle and niece. "I like all the stripes. She sort of reminds me of a faded tiger."

"It's called a brindle coat," he grudgingly explained.

Annalise continued to eye the dog, no longer betraying any sign of fear. Not good. "I wonder what her name is." She squatted next to Isabella. "Maybe if she doesn't have any owners we can name her."

Isabella nodded eagerly and the dog put her sly seal of approval on it by licking first his niece and then his nanny/soon-to-be-strangled-wife-to-be.

"No naming the dog!" he protested.

He might as well have saved his breath. Everyone ignored him. Instead, the three females began a timeless bonding ritual that involved the dog positioned on the floor like a sphinx, while Isabella and Annalise petted her from tongue-lolling head to thumping tail. She whimpered in pathetic gratitude at all the attention while rolling her eyes in his direction. He could have sworn he saw smug laughter lurking there. Oh, yeah. Definitely a sly one. Knew just how to tug at the heartstrings.

"You'd think the guy paying the bills would be the one deserving a petting," he muttered.

"But hell, no. I get to play bad cop. I know how this story ends—with me in the doghouse, while the dog gets all the attention and affection. Well, not this time, bubba. No way, no how."

"What kind of dog is she?" Annalise asked. "Other than big?"

No one was listening to him, or, at least, they'd developed selective hearing. Caving to the inevitable, he examined the animal with a critical eye. "Definitely Great Dane. And judging by the breadth and shape of her, not to mention the droopy ears, I wouldn't be surprised if she had some mastiff mixed in there somewhere."

"Well, whatever she is, she's a beauty," Annalise replied, rocking back onto her heels.

He bent down and retrieved his cell phone from Annalise and punched in the number to the main house. Mrs. Westcott answered on the first ring. "We have a visitor," he explained after they'd exchanged pleasantries. "She's four-legged, about the size of a Humvee. And half-starved."

"You've seen her? Well, thank goodness for that. Animal Control has been trying to catch her for the past week. She's a clever minx, that one is."

He eyed the ecstatic dog who'd rolled onto her back, enjoying a tummy rub, dinner-plate-sized paws pinwheeling in the air. "Well, your clever minx is currently splayed out in the middle of Taye's bungalow living room floor."

"Oh, Mr. Mason. Aren't you sweet to take her in."

"No! No, I'm not—"

"I've been so worried about her. I was just coming to work when I saw her get dumped. A bunch of college kids tossed her out of the car like so much garbage, poor critter. Thank goodness she'll have a good home."

He gritted his teeth. "Only if someone is insane enough to adopt her. Can you call Animal Control for us?" At the question, three pairs of outraged eyes pinned him to the wall. Mrs. Westcott weighed in with a disapproving *tsk*ing sound. "What?" he asked, a shade defensively.

In response, Isabella threw herself on top of the dog as though to prevent anyone from dragging the animal away. He didn't bother to explain that it would take a crane and bulldozer to move the beast if she turned uncooperative.

Annalise moistened her lips, lips he'd taken great delight in kissing only the night before. If she hadn't chosen such an underhanded distraction, his brain cells would have stayed where they belonged instead of draining out of his ears and puddling on the floor.

"Maybe we should discuss this first, before you make any rash decisions." She didn't phrase it like a suggestion. In fact, it sounded suspiciously like a demand. "I don't see why we can't keep her until you track down the owners."

"Is that your new nanny?" Mrs. Westcott asked. "She sounds like a sensible woman."

With the female-to-male ratio running three-to-one against him—he eyed the dog—no, make that four-to-one—the odds were definitely not in his favor. "I never make rash decisions," he announced in a no-nonsense tone of voice. "And considering I'm the one in charge around here, I believe that makes me best qualified to decide whether or not it's appropriate to call Animal Control."

Mrs. Westcott snorted.

"It would only be for a day," Annalise stated, sounding far too authoritative for an employee. "Two, at most."

"There's a simple way to resolve this," Jack said.

He thanked the housekeeper for her assistance and snapped the phone closed with a decisive *click* before approaching the dog and examining the rabies tag. Sure enough, it listed the address and phone number of the clinic where the shot had been administered. He placed the call and within minutes was handed off to the veterinarian.

"I know the dog you mean. Dane/mastiff mix," the vet said, confirming Jack's guess. "That's Madam. She is—or perhaps more accurately based on what you're telling me—*was* the mascot for a college fraternity. They weren't supposed to have her and were told not to bring her back. Apparently, they played several rounds of beer pong in order to determine who'd be the one taking her home. The boy who lost is the one who brought her in. I gather his parents insisted before she moved in."

"I don't suppose you have a name or phone number?"

"I do, for all the good it'll do you. How does the last name 'Zur,' first name 'Lou,' strike you?"

"Lou Zur?" Jack groaned. "Loser?"

"Hmm. Clever lads, these college boys. It gives me such hope for the future of our country. You can check the home number he gave, but it's probably a local bar or strip joint. My guess is that when the boy showed up at home with Madam his parents changed their mind about keeping her. Dumping the dog must have been his brilliant solution to the problem. I wish I could claim his behavior was the exception, but if you visited an animal shelter, you'd see it isn't."

"Is there anything else you can tell me?" Jack asked.

The sound of rustling papers drifted through the receiver. "I can tell you that Madam is approximately two and a half years old, in excellent health and all her shots are up-to-date."

"Thank you. I appreciate your assistance."

"If you plan on adopting her, I can fax you her medical records."

"I'll let you know." He disconnected the call and swore beneath his breath. Now what? He turned and faced Annalise and Isabella, wincing at the undisguised hope gleaming in their eyes. They must have guessed from what little they'd heard that all had not gone well. Or rather, it had gone extremely well…for them.

"The dog's name is Madam," he stalled.

"What about the owner?" Annalise asked. "Did the vet have any contact information?"

He didn't have a choice. He gave her the facts in short, terse sentences and then handed down his final edict. It was the only logical choice and he made his decision crystal-clear and without exceptions or loopholes, question or qualification. And he used his most intimidating tone of voice, the one that left his employees trembling. The tone that had his various vice presidents and board members scrambling to obey. The tone that no one had dared to openly defy in the decade he'd spent building his empire.

"We are going to turn this dog over to the shelter," he pronounced. "End of discussion."

Annalise didn't so much as quiver, let alone tremble. And there wasn't the slightest inkling of a scramble. Instead she shot a pointed look in Isabella's direction before folding her arms across her chest in open defiance. "I think we should consider keeping Madam. She might help with certain adjustment issues."

Didn't she get it? He didn't argue with employees. He spoke; they obeyed. "Help in what way?" he argued. "By eating us out of house and home? By scaring my neighbors? What if that animal drives off Sara and Brett? I can barely keep a nanny as it is. Now you want to deprive me of my housekeeper and handyman, too?"

"I'm sure they'll both fall in love with Madam." Beside her, Isabella nodded eagerly. "Plus, helping to take care of a dog will teach your niece responsibility." Annalise lowered her voice, knocking the final nail into his coffin with a husky plea. "And maybe it'll help with her grief."

"You... I..." He ground his teeth together. "This isn't a conversation to have in front of Isabella and you damn well know it," he informed Annalise.

"Language."

"Oh, you're going to hear some language, just as soon as I get you alone."

"I don't think it's wise to leave Madam unattended with Isabella," Annalise objected, the wicked twinkle in her eye at direct odds with the demureness of her expression. "Not until we know that it's safe."

"Exactly." He seized on the excuse. He pointed toward Madam. "That animal is too big. She could accidently injure Isabella."

"So far she's been very gentle. Not to mention protective. And if she was raised at a dorm, she's accustomed to being around young people."

"We don't know if the mutt is housebroken. Look at the size of her. In case you're unaware of it, there's a distinct correlation between the size of an animal and the size of its steaming piles of sh—" He broke off at Annalise's warning look. "Chunks of chocolate, not to mention the lakes of pi— Son of a bi—" It was all he could do not to rip his hair out by the roots. "Geysers of ginger ale. Who's going to clean that up?"

Honey-gold eyes brimmed with laughter. "We'll make sure Madam gets frequent walks until we're certain she won't accidently leave any chocolate treats or ginger-ale geysers around the house."

"And that's another thing," he was quick to point out. "Who's going to walk her? We'll need a private trucking service to pick up all she dumps along the way."

"That's the purpose of pooper scoopers. We'll manage."

"Not only that, but she's a lot of dog to control. We live in the city. If she gets away from you she might break a car or knock over a power pole or mistake a policeman for a chew toy. Or…or eat some tourists—not that that would be so bad."

Isabella began to giggle, the sound the most delicious thing he'd ever heard in his entire life. "She won't fit in the Jag," he added weakly, struggling to steel himself against that sweet, sweet laugh. "She'll knock over the furniture. The house is full of priceless antiques, you know. She'll probably dig holes straight through to China in my backyard, holes Isabella could fall into. Isabella doesn't speak Chinese."

"She doesn't speak at all," Annalise reminded him. "Maybe Madam can help change that."

He couldn't allow the forlorn hope to sway him. "And the barking. Do you know how much it'll cost to replace the windows the creature's barking will break?"

"I have it on excellent authority that you can afford it." She gazed up at him with eyes capable of melting even his heart of stone. "Please, Jack. Please, can we keep her?"

His niece deserted the dog and flung herself against him, wrapping her arms around his legs and squeezing for all she was worth. "Aw, hell," he muttered.

"I take it we have a dog?" Annalise asked.

"That isn't a dog."

"Elephant...dog...chocolate-and-ginger-ale factory..." She shrugged. "Is she ours?"

He blew out a sigh. "I don't see that I have a choice. Looks like we've just adopted a Madam."

Six

Looking back, Jack realized that Madam's arrival in their lives changed everything. Much to his relief, he discovered that she was definitely housebroken. But she was also a total klutz.

"I'm going to owe Taye a fortune in repairs," he complained to Annalise as he swept up the latest Madam mayhem. "That tail of hers should be registered as a deadly weapon."

"You can't fool me, Mason," Annalise replied. She held the dustpan for him, then emptied the remains of the lamp into the trash can. "Admit it. You adore Madam."

He glanced toward the living room where Isabella and the dog were curled up on the couch together. "What I adore is the change in Isabella since Madam arrived."

To his concern, tears welled up in Annalise's eyes. "She's blossomed, hasn't she?"

"Oh, yeah." He wished he'd been able to bring about such a notable change in his niece, but he'd take it however it happened. The important thing was Isabella's recovery. "I've also sicced my PI on the boys who dumped her. When I track them down, I intend to explain the error of their ways in terms they won't ever forget."

"Good." She glared with unexpected ruthlessness. "I don't suppose you have the power to arrange for them to volunteer at their local animal shelter? Maybe that will underscore the lesson."

"Trust me. I'll find a way to make it happen." He grimaced, turning his attention to more immediate matters. "Now all I have to do is figure out how to keep that four-legged disaster from laying waste to my home."

She caught her lip between her teeth, a frown forming between her eyebrows. "What are you going to do?"

"I've already done it." He'd given the matter a lot of thought before reaching a decision and calling his housekeeper with instructions. "I asked Sara to arrange to have most of the furniture and antiques put into storage for the time being."

Annalise gave him an odd look. "Generations of Mason antiques? You'd put them in storage so Isabella can have a dog?"

"Hell, yes. Trust me, it'll make a vast improvement. That place isn't kid friendly, let alone dog friendly. I should have made the change when Isabella first came to live with me." He took the trash can from her and carried it into the kitchen. "I can remember tiptoeing around that mausoleum when my grandmother lived there, afraid if I breathed wrong I might break some Louis the Umpteenth or Early American Irreplaceable. That's no way for a little girl to live."

"No," Annalise agreed softly. A wobbly smile broke across her face. "It's not. Thank you for putting her best interests first."

"Of course I'm putting her best interests first," he retorted, insulted. "Did you think I wouldn't?"

"At first, perhaps." She offered a self-conscious shrug. "You do have a reputation, Jack. And it's not the sort that suggests you'd be indulgent toward the vagaries of a child. I have to admit I was concerned when I read you'd taken custody of your niece."

He stiffened. "Were you?"

She must have realized it wasn't the most tactful remark she could have made because she winced. "You felt duty bound to take her in, didn't you?"

He couldn't deny it. "Yes."

He watched her choose her words with care. "Some in your position might believe that giving Isabella a home fulfilled that duty. A more unfeeling man would turn her over to a nanny with a clear conscience and go back to business as usual."

An arctic wind blew across his soul. "Most who know me would describe me as just that sort of man. It's who my father raised me to be." Why couldn't she see that? Couldn't she sense the coldness in him, the absence of any ability to love? He was driven to ask, needed to see himself through her eyes. "What makes you think I'm not like that?"

She grinned, her eyes full of warm, golden sunshine. "I've had an opportunity to get to know you. Just in the short time we've been together, I can tell you're not that sort of man."

"You're wrong. I'm exactly that sort of man." He couldn't explain why he was driven to argue the point, other than he needed her to face reality, to see him for who and what he was. "That's why I hired you. I wanted someone who could take care of my niece, leaving me free to get back to living my life on my terms."

She waved his confession aside as thought it were of no concern. "Maybe at first. But as soon as you set eyes on your niece, you changed your mind. You're happy to take an active role in Isabella's life."

"I am?"

Her grin widened. "You're here, aren't you? And you've told me you'll do whatever it takes to retain custody of her. Why do you think you're doing that? It's because you're a softy at heart."

"That's a damn lie. You take it back right now."

She swept him a mocking bow. "Of course, Mr. Mason. I absolutely take it back. After all, you're only a man who's taken in his niece when she had no one else, taken a leave of absence from a multi-billion-dollar company in order to spend time with her, adopted a stray dog, stripped his possessions from his house to accommodate said dog and niece. Why, I've never met anyone more deserving of the name Scrooge."

"That's me. Just call me Ebenezer."

Annalise shot him a sparkling look. "So, tell

me, Eb. Is there anything you wouldn't do for Isabella?"

"No, there isn't." Time to turn the tables. "But I suspect the eventual question will be... Is there anything *you* wouldn't do?"

Annalise's amusement faded. "What do you mean?"

"One of these days I'm going to ask you for a favor that will help my niece," he warned. "I just wonder how you'll answer when that time comes."

She didn't hesitate. "That's easy." To his surprise, she returned his gaze with one weighted with grim determination. "I'll do whatever it takes, too."

He nodded in satisfaction. "Good answer. And just so you know..." He leaned in. Unable to help himself, he brushed her mouth with his, reveling in the brief flash of heat. "I intend to hold you to that promise."

Their remaining days at the bungalow took on a surreal quality. As Jack had warned, the dog threatened to eat them out of house and home. Within days she put on enough weight to hide her painfully thin rib cage, though Jack suspected that might also have something to do with the treats Annalise and Isabella were sneaking the dog whenever his back was turned.

The days flashed by, exhausting, exhilarating and filled with warmth and laughter and plain, old-fashioned fun. He'd never seen Isabella so carefree, even though she still refused to speak. Between Annalise and Madam she was mothered to within an inch of her life.

Not that he was left out of the mix. As often as his niece could be found in Annalise's arms or sprawled across Madam's back, she spent an equal amount of time curled up in his lap. He hoped their familial connection helped heal her grief the way it helped heal his. Their time together seemed to be making a difference, but he could still sense an undercurrent of sorrow that he had no idea how to reach, let alone assuage. As though sensing his mixed emotions, Madam would rumble over to rest her huge head on his knee and offer licks of re-assurance while Annalise watched with her in-candescent smile. That smile made him long for something else, something more. Some-thing that would complete their family unit.

But the true breakthrough happened one morning shortly before they were scheduled to leave. The sun had barely broken the plane of the horizon when his bedroom door banged open and the next instant his mattress over-flowed with dog, niece, doll and a huge picture book that smacked him square in the jaw as Isabella snuggled down next to him.

"Baby Belle?" he asked sleepily. "What's wrong?"

She shoved the book into his hands and patted it, blinking up at him with absurdly long lashes. Her dimple flashed. Madam settled her huge head on his spare pillow with a wide yawn and promptly went back to sleep.

"You want me to read to you?" Jack asked. She nodded, leaning her head against his chest. Her halo of curls, still pillow-ruffled, were downy soft and seemed to have a mind of their own. A sudden memory came to him. "This is…this is Family Bed, isn't it?" he asked gruffly.

She nodded and patted the book again. Before he could gather himself sufficiently to read, he heard Annalise shuffling in the general direction of his niece's bedroom.

"Isabella? Madam? Hey, where is everyone?"

"She's in here," he called. "We're all in here."

Annalise appeared in the doorway, her curls as tumbled and ruffled as his niece's. She pulled up short at the sight of all of them piled in his bed. "Oh," she said, disconcerted. "There you are. What…what are you doing?"

"It's Family Bed," he offered.

She blinked at him in utter bewilderment. "What's Family Bed?"

And he'd thought he'd been deprived. He wondered why she'd never experienced something so wondrous. What had her childhood been like that she'd never known the pleasure of curling up with her parents and siblings in one big bed? Even he, with his dearth of close family ties had, for one sweet summer, known the joy of Family Bed.

"Every Sunday my mother, stepfather, and Joanne would collect books and newspapers, coffee and juice, and spend the first couple of hours of the day in bed together." He glanced down at his niece, tucked close to his side. "I gather Joanne continued the tradition."

A wistful smile teased at the corners of Annalise's mouth. "It sounds lovely."

"Why don't you join us?"

A sweeping flash of vulnerability betrayed her longing to do just that and made Jack think of a child with her nose pressed to the candy store window, always on the outside looking in. Never allowed a taste of heaven. He'd had close and personal experience with that particular emotion, having iced up his nose on that window on more than one occasion. Then her expression vanished as though it had never been, and he could only marvel at her self-control.

"I don't think it would be appropriate for me to join you." She edged toward the door. "I'll just get breakfast started while you and Isabella enjoy reading together."

"We can fix breakfast later on. Right now it's time for Family Bed." He nudged his niece. "Isn't that right?"

She nodded eagerly and held out her arms to Annalise, who wavered, clearly torn between a desire to share in something she'd never encountered before and longed to experience, and maintaining a professional distance.

"Come on, Stefano. You're needed here."

He'd said the exact right thing. Her smile nearly blinded him as she approached the bed. He grabbed Madam by her collar and wrestled her toward the end of the mattress in order to give Annalise room. She slid beneath the covers next to Isabella and the three of them reclined side by side, against mounds of pillows. He opened the Mrs. Pennywinkle book and cleared his throat.

"'It was a cold winter day when the magical china doll, Nancy, found her way to the next little girl who needed her...'" he began.

Beside him, his niece patted her doll's back and hugged her closer. "Your doll looks just like the one in the book," Annalise said in surprise. "Is...is she a Nancy doll?" At Isabella's nod, a husky tone entered her voice. "No wonder she's so special. Do you think she's here to help you like the doll in your story-book?"

Again Isabella nodded, this time pointing to the dog. "You think your Nancy doll sent Madam to you?" Jack asked. When his niece nodded a third time, more emphatically, he exchanged an uneasy glance with Annalise. "Is this going to be a problem?"

"I don't think so, not unless she starts to believe that her doll can grant wishes."

"And if that's what she already believes?"

"I don't know," Annalise admitted. "I guess we hope that with the proper amount of love and attention and counseling, she gradually realizes that isn't the case. I have to admit, I'm a little out of my depth on this one."

Isabella gave the book an impatient tap and Jack forced himself to relax and offer an apologetic smile. "Sorry, munchkin. I got distracted there. What do you say we start over?"

The next hour passed on wings, ending too soon as far as Jack was concerned. When his bed emptied out so that everyone could dress, so did the warmth, and he decided then and there that Family Bed would become a weekly ritual from this point forward. His cell phone rang just as Annalise herded Isabella toward the kitchen to whip up a batch of pancakes. He checked caller ID and connected the call.

"Yeah, Derek. What's up?"

"Sorry to call so early in the morning, but the PI's preliminary report just hit my in-box and I knew you'd like the results ASAP."

"And?"

"And Ms. Stefano is clean…for the most part."

Jack spared a quick glance toward the hallway. Girlish laughter slipped out from the direction of the kitchen and he nudged his door closed. "What part isn't so clean?"

"There was a small matter when she was sixteen. Cops raided some kid's birthday bash and issued her a citation for underage drinking. They expunged her record after she completed some court-ordered community service. Since then, she's been so clean she squeaks."

Jack lowered his voice. "If the record was expunged, how did you get the details?"

"I have my sources. I'm not minimizing what she did, Jack, but it was a long time ago. Her mother had died a couple years before that and her father was in the military at the time. After her brush with the law, he took an early discharge and started up a fishing charter service, I'm guessing so he could assume a more hands-on role. He sent her off each summer to stay with an aunt during tourist season. The aunt's a school teacher who lives out near Columbia. She's probably the one who influenced Annalise's career choice."

"Did you find anything that might concern CPS?"

"Nothing. I doubt they'll even dig up as much as I have." There was a brief pause. "So, how's it going at your end? Your marriage project moving right along?" he asked a shade too casually.

"It's coming."

"Coming…as in soon, though, right?"

Jack let out a long sigh. He knew that tone. "Aw, hell. What do you know that I don't?"

"The Locke woman's making noises again. I've done everything I can to have her replaced, but apparently she's irreplaceable."

"How much time do I have?" Jack asked grimly.

"Let's see…. Soon would be good. If you and your charming bride-to-be were to show up at the

Judicial Center and fill out a marriage application sometime today, you could be wedded and bedded in twenty-four hours. How does that sound?"

"Hell, Derek. That isn't soon. That's immediate."

"Immediate works for me."

"Well, it doesn't for me. And I guarantee, it won't for Annalise."

"I strongly suggest you find a way for it to work for both of you. Once you're officially married, I can probably hold off CPS for another month or so, convince them the two of you deserve time to settle into connubial bliss. But that's as far as I'll be able to push it. You need to marry now in order for me to insist on any sort of further delay. And then you need to create a loving relationship that's good enough to pass Mrs. Locke's scrutiny."

Jack closed his eyes and ran a hand along the nape of his neck. Damn it to hell. "I'll try."

"I suggest you do more than try."

Jack spent the rest of the day considering and rejecting any number of arguments to present to Annalise, everything from a declaration of undying love—which would leave her laughing herself silly—to the unvarnished truth, which he feared would not only leave him without a bride but without a nanny, as well.

Still… What choice did he have? He couldn't lie to her. He slanted her a calculating look as they put Isabella down for the night. He needed to find a way to convince his nanny to agree to a coldly logical, if highly offensive, proposal of marriage. But, how?

There was only one way. He'd tell her the truth and hope she'd been serious when she had claimed she'd do everything in her power to help Isabella. "We need to talk," he informed her, as soon as they finished tucking in his niece.

Annalise regarded him with a worried frown. "Is something wrong?"

He waited until they'd returned to the living room before explaining. "According to my lawyer, I need to marry immediately in order to retain custody of Isabella."

She stared in shock. "Oh, Jack, is he certain?"

"Very." He gave it to her straight. "Derek's held endless conversations with Mrs. Locke and various officials at CPS. Though they haven't come right out and said I must have a wife, they're extremely concerned that between my work schedule and Isabella's issues I'm not the best person to raise her. There's even been some discussion about placing her in a treatment facility. I won't let that happen, which means I present them with an acceptable wife who can give Isabella the attention she requires when I'm not available."

Annalise stared at him, stunned. "But…who are you going to marry? Does Isabella know her? Does she even like her?"

"She adores her."

That brought her up short. "Oh. Well… Well,

that's good. I don't quite know what else to say," she added weakly. "Congratulations?"

"She hasn't accepted my offer yet."

Annalise stilled. "Wait a minute. Is this your way of telling me you no longer need my services?" A look of utter devastation swept across her face. "Is your wife—assuming she accepts your offer—is she going to take care of Isabella full-time?"

"Yes and no. I still need your services." Jack captured an escaped curl, one that tumbled halfway down Annalise's back, and used it to reel her in. "Just in a slightly different capacity. I hope you'll consider it a promotion."

She was quick to put two and two together and come up with the requisite four. He watched shock etch a path across her elegant features. "You don't mean… You can't possibly think I—"

"Oh, but I can and I do. Ms. Stefano, I would very much appreciate it if you'd consider exchanging your position as nanny for one as my wife."

The couch caught her as her knees gave out. "You can't be serious."

"I'm dead serious. You may recall that I once told you that I'd do whatever it took to retain custody of Isabella. I also seem to remember you saying something quite similar. I know how serious I was when I made that statement. How serious were you?"

Pain burst to life in her eyes, burning with an intensity that seared straight through to his soul. He accepted it, didn't attempt to defend against it. He deserved to burn for what he was about to do. And no doubt he would.

"Oh, Jack," she whispered. "How could you?"

He captured Annalise's hands in his and drew her to her feet again. "As I've informed you more than once, I will do whatever it takes to retain custody of Isabella. But I will also do whatever you ask, give you whatever you demand, in exchange for your agreement to my plan. Please, Annalise. Marry me."

"No." She shook her head, the restlessness of

her curls revealing the extent of her distress. "I can't. Anything but that."

"You're not already married?" Surely the PI would have uncovered evidence of a husband.

"No, of course not."

"And you claimed you weren't involved with anyone."

"I'm not."

"Then it's a moral objection."

She gazed at him helplessly. "You don't understand."

He cupped her face, drew her upward so their mouths met, colliding in soft passion, igniting sparks he didn't dare allow to catch fire. "Then explain it to me so I will."

It took her a moment to gather her wits enough to reply. "I adore Isabella, you know that. I'd do anything to ensure her recovery. But it would be wrong for me to agree to this, wrong on so many levels."

"It would be temporary, Annalise. Once CPS signs off, you're free to leave whenever you want. I'll make sure you're provided for."

"You mean money," she said bluntly. "You mean, you'll pay me to be your wife."

He'd never been accused of being a charming man, so he didn't bother trying to act the part. "I believe it's called alimony. But if you'd prefer to consider it wages—just like you're paid wages as Isabella's nanny—that's fine with me."

Her chin quivered. "Well, it's not fine with me."

"Because of the money or because you think it's wrong?"

"I don't know." Her voice broke and she covered her face with her hands. "I just don't know."

"Listen to me. I'm not paying you for sex. If you choose to share my bed, it's because we're attracted to each other physically. Consider this an old-fashioned, arranged marriage. I'm a man with a child in need of a wife and mother. You're a woman who has career goals which can more easily be met as a result of our marriage."

She bowed her head and he waited for endless moments while she weighed her options. Finally, she spoke, her voice whisper-soft. "My father once told me that being a single parent was the most difficult job he'd ever attempted. He never felt he'd done a proper job. The guilt ate him alive."

Jack forced himself to use her admission, hating himself even as he said the words. "I won't have that guilt or those concerns, if you marry me."

Her hands dropped to her sides and he could see tears welling into her eyes. "How long?" she whispered.

"Figure a couple of years, tops."

Pain ripped through her gaze again. "And then you expect me to simply walk away?"

"You were going to walk away regardless, remember?" he reminded her softly. "You agreed to a two-year contract while you pursued your master's, and then you were going to teach."

Her gaze strayed in the direction of Isabella's room and a hint of panic deepened the intense color of her irises, turning them to amber. "This job is just temporary." She said it almost as though reminding herself of that fact. "I know that."

"All I'm suggesting is that you spend those two years as my wife instead of Isabella's nanny."

For once her self-control deserted her, leaving her open and defenseless. "It won't be easy for her when I leave. We'll have grown attached."

"I won't cut you off. I lived that existence, remember? I wouldn't do that to my niece any more than I'd do that to you. We'll make the transition as slowly and gently as possible. I won't prevent Isabella from seeing you whenever she wants."

To his concern, her tears escaped, streaking down her cheeks. "I wasn't supposed to become attached."

"We'll work it out. You have my word. But all this will be moot if CPS takes Isabella from me."

For some reason, reminding her of that fact got through as nothing else had. She bowed her head and scrubbed the heels of her palms across her cheeks. "She belongs with you," Annalise whispered. "She needs you. I want to do whatever I can to cement your relationship with her. That was the whole point in taking this job."

"Then marry me. I swear you won't regret it."

"Yes, I will." She looked at him. "I'll probably regret it for the rest of my life. But I don't think I have any choice."

The first time he'd seen her, he'd thought her eyes overflowed with ancient wisdom and intense vulnerability. Tonight they also reflected a gut-wrenching devastation. She'd suffered in the past, he sensed, even more than he had. He found he wanted to know her, to dig down through all that pain and uncover her most deeply guarded secrets. As though sensing the direction of his thoughts, shutters snapped closed over her expression and she took a step backward.

"Very well, Jack. I accept your proposal," she said. "I'll marry you and do whatever I can to convince CPS to give you full custody of your niece."

He closed the distance between them, unwilling to allow her to shut him out. They may have chosen to enter their marriage in a cold-blooded fashion, but it wouldn't continue that way. He slid his hands around her waist and tipped her into his arms. She fell against him, all feminine softness and delicious warmth.

"Don't," she pleaded. "It's too much for me to handle."

"Handle?" He lifted an eyebrow. "Or control?"

"Either. Both."

"Then let go. I'll take care of everything."

He lowered his head and took her mouth. It was a simple kiss, yet one that created an intense explosion of pleasure. She struggled for a brief instant, more against herself than him. And then she wrapped her arms around his neck and sank into the heat.

He wished he could claim that he was kissing her for Isabella's sake. But it would have been a lie. Selfishly, he wanted her for himself. Wanted it all. Wanted to right the world for his niece and try to give her some measure of happiness. And he wanted this woman in his bed, to wake beside her each morning. Endless Sundays filled with Family Bed stretched out before him, the mattress overflowing with child and dog, husband and wife. It was a life he'd never known.

It was a life he'd do whatever was necessary to create.

Seven

The wedding ceremony took place two short days later. It had been a struggle to convince Annalise that a formal wedding gown and tux was an absolute necessity. When he suggested as much, she'd stared at him in horrified disbelief.

"You must be joking."

"Not even a little. Think it through logically, Annalise. This needs to be convincing. The unfortunate fact is, my name is going to generate news. Our marriage is going to generate news. I intend to use that to our advantage. I want every newspaper, rag and media outlet to splash lots of pictures of us in formal wedding gear. I want all the articles to rave about the whirlwind romance between the ruthless tycoon and the adorable nanny who won his heart."

She paled. "My father. He has no idea I even work for you. What am I supposed to tell him about our marriage?"

"Tell him it was love at first sight."

"He'll never believe that."

Jack's eyes narrowed. "Why not?"

"He just won't," she argued. "He knows me. He knows I'm not the type to fall for someone like you."

"Someone like me?" He wondered if he sounded as offended as he felt.

"Rich. Powerful." She regarded him impatiently, refusing to reflect even a modicum of nervousness at his reaction. "It's too fast. I'm a cautious type of person."

"What's really going on, Annalise?"

Her chin shot up. "You once told me your

father taught you to do whatever it takes to achieve your goals. Well, mine taught me not to make rash decisions. Just as you've taken your family motto to heart, so have I. My father knows I wouldn't marry someone I've only known for a couple of weeks."

"Then you'll have to find a way to convince him that you've made an exception this one time."

She spun away, turning her back to him so he couldn't read her expression. "Dad agreed to captain a charter into the Caribbean for the summer. It may take a while to track down his boat and get word through to him. This is something that needs to be done in person. When he does get in touch, I'll do my best to convince him it's a love match, but I suggest we come up with an alternative story. Because I guarantee we're going to need one." She faced Jack once again. She'd gathered up her self-control and hid every scrap of emotion behind a calm expression. "How will your father react to our marriage?"

"I guess we'll find out when it hits the news-papers."

Her air of calm evaporated. "You're not going to tell him yourself?"

He bared his teeth in a grin. "Trust me. It'll be more fun if we do it my way."

He didn't give her time to argue the situation. Instead he dropped her and Isabella off at an ex-clusive little boutique with instructions to the proprietor to dress his bride-to-be in the most romantic gown available, and to make sure that his niece wore something that matched. The blank check he offered to make certain every-thing was completed on time ensured satisfac-tion on behalf of both parties. Much to his private amusement, he left Isabella glowing and Annalise glowering.

The next morning Derek had surprised him by showing up on his doorstep with Taye McClin-tock in tow.

"What the hell…?" Jack greeted his two best friends with a broad grin.

"Fine greeting *that* is," Taye griped. "I fly in all the way from Singapore—"

"I thought you were in Paris."

"That was last month." Taye paused, and his angel's face assumed a wicked expression. "Doesn't really matter, does it? I couldn't miss your wedding, could I?"

Jack spared Derek a brief glance. "You told him?" he asked.

"About the wedding, yes."

"About the reason for it, no," Taye contributed with the comfortable brazenness of an old friend. "But I can make a fairly good guess. And I'm guessing that it has something to do with Isabella and that ongoing fight you're having with CPS. Am I right?"

Jack started to agree, then for reasons he didn't dare analyze, he hesitated. "Isabella's part of the reason," he grudgingly admitted.

He couldn't explain his reluctance to go into the finer points, but suspected it had something to do with Annalise. Even though Derek had drawn up the prenup that spelled out every last detail of their forthcoming marriage, he felt a bone-deep urge to protect his bride from his two best friends, which struck him as vaguely ludicrous. Even so, he didn't want them to think she was marrying him for financial gain, mainly because he knew that wasn't her true reason. Like him, she was simply putting Isabella first, and that fact had to be protected and celebrated.

Derek's eyes narrowed. "Well, well. Who'd have thought?"

"Thought what?" Jack asked defensively.

"That the great Jack Mason has been brought to his knees by his nanny."

"Stuff it, Fletcher. It isn't like that."

"Huh." Taye appeared intrigued. "I think it's exactly like that. I don't doubt Isabella is a big part of the reason for the hasty marriage, but I think you have a thing for your bride-to-be." Before Jack could argue the point, he added, "But, the more interesting question is why the hell would she marry you, Mason?"

Jack felt his anger stir. "If that's the attitude you two are going to adopt, you can support me on my wedding day by taking off."

Taye chuckled. "Oh, yeah. I can definitely see the appeal now."

"You know…" Derek chimed in, "Taye raises an interesting point. I thought she was marrying you for the obvious reasons." He and Taye exchanged a knowing look and chimed in together, "Money."

"You don't think she is?" Taye asked.

"Guys—"

Derek shrugged. "I'm not so sure. When I met with her yesterday, I didn't read 'gold digger,' if you know what I mean."

Jack lost his patience. "That's because she isn't."

"Which brings us back to Taye's point." Derek lifted a sooty eyebrow. "Precisely why *is* she marrying you, Jack? For Isabella's sake? Fast work, that. What in the world would prompt a woman to sacrifice two years of her life for a child she barely knows?"

"Unless it was for money." Taye slipped the suggestion in again with far too much cynicism. But then, he had cause, as Jack knew all too well. A small case of been there/done that. "If it wasn't for the money…" Taye allowed the comment to trail off.

Jack shrugged uneasily. "She cares about Isabella, just as I do. She plans to get her master's over the next two years, and this will provide her with the perfect opportunity to set herself up for the future while helping Isabella."

It sounded weak, even to his ears. As though sensing his concern, his friends exchanged meaningful looks and deliberately changed the subject. Jack listened with half an ear. Now that he stopped to consider the matter, he had to admit that his plan to circumvent CPS had fallen into place with impressive ease. Granted, he'd always had a knack for getting his own way and making things come together to his advantage. This was just one more example of that, right? But he couldn't stop the question from fomenting in the back of his mind.

Why *had* Annalise really agreed to marry him? Was it for Isabella's sake, as she claimed? Or did she have a very different agenda?

The wedding itself took place late that afternoon in the serenity of his backyard, with Taye and Derek at his side. Annalise and Isabella walked together across the lawn toward him, hand in hand, while a string quartet played softly and a photographer worked discreetly in the background. His bride paused halfway to the makeshift altar and stooped to adjust his niece's hat. Dappled sunlight framed them, capturing them within a golden glow. And just like that, his heart stopped.

In that moment, his wife-to-be had to be the most beautiful woman he'd ever seen. Her hair had been pulled back from her face and allowed to tumble in an abandoned riot of curls down her back. Her wispy veil was anchored in place by a circlet of gold and silver, the craftsmanship of the leaf-and-diamond-encrusted piece drawing attention to her vivid eyes. Her ivory gown was perfectly suited to her tall, lean figure, the bodice fitted, the sweeping skirt complemented by a long flowing train. She looked like a fantasy creature from another era, and yet he knew just how real she was.

Isabella also wore an ivory gown with lace insets that matched the trim on Annalise's wedding gown. As far as Jack was concerned, his niece resembled nothing more than a small angel. Instead of a veil, she wore an adorable wide-brimmed bonnet that framed her apple-cheeked face. Gold-tipped brown ringlets peeked out from the edges and bobbed in the gentle breeze. She beamed with excitement.

Instead of carrying her Nancy doll—something he rarely saw her without—she held a basket full of ivory and blush-pink roses. Then, much to his amusement, he noticed the doll perched at the base of the tree near where he was standing. He grinned. His adorable niece had dressed the doll for the occasion in a gown and bonnet that, even to his untrained eye, appeared identical to the one Isabella wore.

An instant later, the two joined him beneath the weighty fuchsia blossoms of a crape myrtle, and the minister spoke the traditional opening words that would soon join them together as husband and wife. The ceremony took no time at all. One minute he was a man who'd sworn never to take a wife. The next instant he was married to a woman who gazed at him with such a wealth of emotion that it took every ounce of self-control to keep himself from sweeping her into his arms and carrying her off to where they could spend the next twenty-four hours in un-interrupted seclusion.

That wasn't part of the plan, he reminded himself. This marriage had nothing to do with his new bride and everything to do with the child standing at their side. And he'd do well to remember that.

The minister cut across his thoughts, speaking the timeless words to conclude the ceremony. "You may now kiss the bride."

Jack didn't require any further prompting. He cupped Annalise's face and tilted it upward. Her veil fluttered like a flag of surrender, while her curls shivered in protest. But her eyes, those glorious honey-gold eyes, gazed at him with undisguised want. Was she even aware of how much they gave away? He doubted it. If she had the least suspicion, she'd have done everything in her power to tuck the truth away behind that serene facade she clung to with such determination. He hoped Taye and Derek didn't notice her expression. That was his, and his alone, something he refused to share with anyone else.

Slowly he lowered his head and captured her mouth. Her lips were softer than the roses in Isabella's basket and tasted of sunshine and warmth. He filled his hands with the glorious weight of her hair and the silken curls twined around his fingers, anchoring them together. She sighed against his mouth, the sound one of sweet surrender. If he could have gathered up all the various scents and sounds and tastes and preserved them for all time, he would have given his fortune to do so. But moments like this didn't last, and their kiss was no exception.

From the direction of the house a great booming *woof* broke the spell and the ground shook beneath their feet. Madam erupted from the kitchen and spilled onto the patio. Catching sight of the three of them, she gave her widest, most delighted grin and charged across the lawn.

The minister uttered a word that Jack was fairly certain couldn't be found anywhere in the Bible he held and scurried behind the nearest tree. The string quartet grabbed their instruments and made a beeline for the gate exiting from the yard, toppling chairs in their haste to escape. Taking a cue from them, the minister made a speedy departure, as well. Only Taye, Derek and the photographer didn't budge. While his friends burst into shouts of laughter, the photographer simply kept snapping pictures as the beast joined in the festivities.

With a thundering bark of excitement, Madam reared back and lunged at Jack, felling him with one blow. Unfortunately, his hands were still anchored in Annalise's hair. She tumbled onto the grass beside him, in a tangled heap of silk and lace. Isabella launched herself at Madam, attempting to pull the dog off them. It was like watching a kitten attempt to subdue a moose. She ended up riding Madam like a pony, her bonnet turned half sideways, her dainty skirts hitched to her knees.

Beside him he felt Annalise's shoulders tremble and a muffled sound escaped, something that sounded suspiciously like a sob. "Are you hurt?" He tried to find her through all the lace, satin and tulle. "Sweetheart, please don't cry. It'll be all right."

She managed to push aside her veil and a heavy swath of curls, revealing eyes swimming with tears. But they weren't tears of sorrow or anger. She tilted back her head and burst out laughing. His mouth twitched. And then he was laughing, too.

"So much for a traditional, elegant affair," he muttered.

"Considering ours isn't exactly a traditional family to begin with, it seems quite appropriate to me." Annalise attempted to twitch her skirts into place, skirts that had ridden up high enough to reveal—Lord preserve his sanity—a tantalizing glimpse of a sexy lace garter and a hint of creamy thigh. "And, I hate to disappoint you, but I'm not really cut out for elegant."

Jack leaned in and kissed her, a brief, thorough kiss that left her cheeks glowing and her eyes sparkling. "Do I look disappointed?" He shoved at the dog. "You two are now officially forbidden from sneaking Madam any more treats. She's getting so fat, she's practically waddling.

And as for you two—" He shot his friends a glare that only served to increase their amusement. "Thanks for your help."

Derek offered a broad grin. "Anytime."

"My pleasure," Taye added.

Jack gained his feet and helped his bride to hers. With one stern command, he had Isabella removed from Madam's back and the dog sitting calmly at his heels. The photographer stepped forward.

"Would you like a few formal shots?" His mouth twitched. "I think all the informal poses are covered."

"But we're a mess," Annalise protested.

Jack shook his head. "You look beautiful."

Her amusement faded, replaced by concern. "You wanted this to look good," she explained in a low voice. "I know how important it is."

"It'll be fine. Here, just a few minor adjustments…"

Gravely, he finger-combed her unruly curls into a semblance of order—but not too orderly.

He liked how they rampaged down her back in exuberant disregard. Then he centered the circlet on her brow and straightened her veil. He brushed the bits of grass and debris from her skirts and then nodded in satisfaction.

Isabella tugged at the tails of his tux and regarded him with a worried expression. "Your turn?" he asked gently.

At her solemn nod, he adjusted her bonnet, retying the ribbon beneath her dainty chin. He took his time removing every blade of grass from her skirts and then turned her in a slow circle. He nodded in satisfaction.

"Picture perfect," he said approvingly.

He winked at Annalise, surprised to see tears in her eyes again. This time they weren't from joy. There was bittersweet quality to her expression. Forcing a smile to her lips, she stepped forward to join them. The next half hour passed in a flurry of camera shots, some with Madam, some without. By the time they were finished, afternoon had faded into evening. Taye and

Derek made their farewells, shaking Jack's hand with impressive formality, and kissing the bride with far too much enthusiasm.

"What next?" Annalise asked, once they were alone. She attempted to hide her nervousness with only limited success.

"Sara's prepared a formal dinner for us. I didn't think it wise to go to a hotel in case Isabella has a problem, so we'll be staying here. I've arranged for Mrs. Walters, just in case."

"Oh." To his intense fascination, color came and went in Annalise's face. "Is that really necessary?"

He held her gaze with his. "Without question."

She spared a brief glance in Isabella's direction. His niece was sitting beneath the tree with her Nancy doll. Madam hovered nearby. "I assumed my room would be adjacent to Isabella's and we wouldn't need Mrs. Walters any longer. After all, that's why I'm here."

"You're my wife now. You'll share my room."

Alarm flared to life. "Jack, this isn't a real

marriage," she whispered. "We shouldn't be sharing a bedroom."

"This *is* a real marriage and we *will* share a bedroom *and* a bed." He caught her hand in his and drew her closer, keeping his voice low and reassuring. "CPS will notice if we're not living as husband and wife. So will Sara and Mrs. Walters. Even Isabella will sense that something's off. She's too young to understand what, but I want her to feel safe and secure on every level. Having two parents who act like parents will help her do that."

"We never discussed this aspect of our marriage," she protested. "I assumed—"

He smiled. "You assumed wrong."

"How far do you plan to take this?"

"Take what?"

She regarded him with naked apprehension. "Take our relationship."

"As far as you let me," he answered calmly.

"And if it's not as far as you'd like?" she shot back.

"You draw the line, Annalise, wherever you want it. The real question is—" he snatched a quick kiss that had Isabella giggling "—what will you do when one of us steps over it?"

Dinner that night passed on wings, filled with laughter and delicious food, while the conversation flowed with surprising ease. It wasn't until afterward that time slowed and stuttered. Much to Jack's amusement, Annalise did her best to drag the evening out. Still dressed in their wedding finery—at Isabella's insistence—they played games until bedtime, at which point Mrs. Walters came to collect his niece.

There was a moment of concern when she protested being escorted to bed, but Annalise stepped in with surprising firmness, and Isabella gave them a reluctant hug and kiss before retiring. The instant they were alone, Jack scooped his bride into his arms and carried her to their bedroom.

"This isn't necessary," she protested.

"Indulge me. It's not every day a man marries."

"Jack, please."

"I intend to please you."

He shouldered open the door to the master suite and stepped across the threshold before gently setting his bride on her feet. She stood, unmoving, examining her surrounds with a combination of curiosity and nervousness. He tried to see the room through her eyes.

The furnishings were sturdy pieces with clean, simple lines, stained to a deep golden sheen. They weren't overwhelmingly masculine, yet they were a bit stark. The candles helped, giving the room a warm, welcoming glow. Sara had provided a few romantic touches of her own by scattering a pathway of ivory and blush pink rose petals from the doorway to the bed, as well as across the duvet covering the mattress. Two crystal flutes stood at the ready alongside a bottle of champagne that rested in a bucket of ice. He studied the scene with an uncertainty he'd never experienced in the business world, concerned about Annalise's reaction.

For more years than Jack could count, he'd lived in an emotional wasteland. His father had been a cold bastard and still was, and he treated his son as little more than a commodity.

His mother had left him, though he didn't doubt it had been against her will. Not that it had changed those lonely years of his childhood. And Joanne…God, how he missed her. He'd survived her loss, of course. Barely. But ever since his parents' divorce, he'd learned to keep tight control over all aspects of his life. To hold people at a distance. He had no intention of ever being deserted, physically or emotionally, again.

As though sensing the dark direction of his thoughts, Annalise offered him a tentative smile. "This is lovely," she said. "Like something out of a fairy tale."

With the gift of one simple smile, warmth flooded through him and the cold and dark faded. This was his wife. His woman. It didn't matter how or why they'd come to exchange those vows. In this moment, they belonged together and he'd do whatever necessary to make this night one she never forgot.

"I'm glad you like it." He gestured toward the champagne. "Would you care for a glass?"

"I don't drink," she confessed.

He tilted his head to one side. Interesting, considering Derek's report. "Not at all?"

Her mouth twisted. "I had a small run-in with alcohol when I was sixteen. It didn't agree with me."

"This might be a good time to confess that I already know about the incident."

She froze. "How is that possible?" she asked carefully.

"I have an excellent PI. I had you checked out after I hired you. I believe he referred to it as a youthful indiscretion." He attempted to interpret her reaction to his confession with only limited success. "Are you angry that I had you investigated?"

She drew a cautious breath. "I guess that depends on why you did it."

He didn't hesitate. "I did it to make sure you were a safe and trustworthy person to have around Isabella."

She seemed to breathe a little easier. "Yes, of course. Since we're now married, I assume I checked out?"

"With that one exception." He still couldn't get a read on her and it puzzled him. "Did you want to talk about it?"

She shrugged and wandered across the room to the bow window that overlooked the courtyard where they'd been married. Her gown rustled in the silence of the room. She perched on the edge of the window seat, her skirts settling around her in a graceful arc. Moonlight cascaded through the beveled panes and bathed her in silver, while leaving her expression in shadow.

"There's not much to tell. I got drunk."

"It happens to most of us at one point or another. That's when we learn there's a reason for our current drinking laws." He approached her the way he would a wounded animal, slowly and with utmost caution. "Is there more to it than that?"

She sat without moving and simply stared at him. "To be honest, I don't remember a lot about that night."

A hideous suspicion took hold. "Did someone take advantage of you?" he asked sharply. "Were you drugged?"

"Not exactly. At least, I don't think so," she whispered. "But I did lose my virginity."

Fury consumed him. "You were taken advantage of. What sort of bastard—"

She stopped him with a quick shake of her head. "He was no more capable of making rational decisions than I was. Trust me, he paid a steep price for it."

"I gather your father found out?" Jack guessed.

"And his. It…wasn't pretty."

"I can imagine." It explained so much about her, especially her need to keep herself under such tight control. He closed the remaining distance between them and sat beside her, taking her hand in his. Her fingers were like ice. "Why are you telling me all this, Annalise?"

"Because you should know that I haven't had any alcohol since that night." She lifted her chin and met his gaze with a directness that sliced straight through to his soul. "And I haven't been with anyone sexually since then, either."

The air burned in his lungs and he slowly exhaled. "Never?"

"No."

"Because of one youthful mistake?"

She hesitated, as though considering the matter. "It didn't seem...wise. Plus, I've never really been tempted." Her eyes burned in the darkness. "Until now."

He stilled. He hadn't realized until that moment how desperately he wanted her. But he couldn't take her. Not after what she'd told him. He'd been so cold for so long, had looked forward to warming himself in the fiery heat of Annalise's desire. But he couldn't take advantage of her like that callous boy from her youth. He wouldn't.

He fought for control, fought for the cool, calm deliberation that had once come with such ease. "Annalise—"

"You're going to send me away, aren't you?"

"What?" He shook his head. "No, not away. Just to the room next door."

"I was hoping you'd say that."

He froze at her words. A stinging slap couldn't have made a harsher impact.

"Earlier today I was positive that was what I wanted," she went on. "But I realize now that was just fear speaking."

"Fear?"

"Last time I was sixteen," she explained. "I don't even remember the act itself. Now, the pain? That I recall. The embarrassment when it was over is a particularly vivid memory, not to mention the humiliation when the whispers started during the weeks and months afterward."

He regarded her with compassion. "I'm so sorry."

She shrugged. "I'm not sixteen anymore, Jack. My fear isn't logical. It's more of a wispy memory than a rational emotion." Her mouth curved into a smile full of feminine mystery and wry humor. "Don't you think it's past time I changed all that?"

"Are you certain?"

"I'm positive." She shifted to face him. "Please, Jack. Help me replace those other memories with new ones. Better ones. Special ones."

A short, harsh laugh was torn from him. "But no pressure, right?"

"I'm fairly certain most of the pressure is on me." She disengaged her hand from his and slid her fingers along his arm to his neck. She tugged gently. "Like this, for instance."

He bent closer and allowed her to take charge of the kiss. Her mouth slid across his as light as a whisper. She moved in again, a slow, thorough exploration. Then she slipped inward, giving him a taste of such sweetness that it proved headier than the most potent drink. She eased backward, breaking the contact.

"See what I mean? What if I do something wrong?"

He cleared his throat. "Not a chance."

"No? Why don't we test your theory."

She caught the edges of his bow tie and tugged. The scrap of silk slid away and drifted toward the floor, vanishing into the shadows. One by one she removed the studs from his shirt, placing each in turn on the windowsill in a neat line. His shirt parted. Did she have any clue what her slow, deliberate movements were doing to him? It took every ounce of willpower to allow her to take the lead, to follow instead of dictate.

Her hand slid into his and she turned it in order to have access to his cufflinks. First one and then the other joined his shirt studs on the windowsill. He wanted her hands on his skin, to feel them move on him. Warm him. Take him. Instead, she eased his shirt from his shoulders, not once actually touching him.

His breathing grew harsh. "Anna—"

"Shh. It'll be all right."

With a soft rustle of silk, she stood in front of him and gently lifted the circlet and veil from her head. She placed it on the window seat beside him. The tulle and lace flowed over the edge like a waterfall, a silent statement in the moonlit darkness. Never once taking her eyes from his, she lowered the side zip of the gown.

Inch by glorious inch, the beaded silk fell away, revealing skin beautifully gilded by their weeks at the beach. The gown slipped to the floor in a soft cloud of surrender. She stepped free of it, as well as her voluminous petticoats, and stood before him in a lacy bustier. He leaned back against the coolness of the window with a groan. He'd caught a glimpse of her stockings and garter when Madam had knocked them to the ground, but it hadn't prepared him for this.

"Let me do the rest," he demanded.

He didn't wait for her agreement, but erupted from the window seat. Gathering her into his arms, he kissed her. Claimed her. Told her without words how beautiful he found her. And then he journeyed downward, worshipping her with mouth and tongue and teeth.

Turning her so her back was to him, he swept the ebony tumble of curls over her shoulder and unhooked her bustier, exposing the elegant sweep of her spine. He traced his fingertip from the back of her neck down to the dip just above her buttocks. Teasing her with the lightest of caresses, he finished undressing her until she stood before him clad only in the silvery rays pouring in through the window. She lifted her arms and shook her hair free. The heavy ringlets cascaded toward her waist. Then she turned ever so slightly and looked at him over her shoulder. He could just make out the sweet curve of her breast.

"Please, Jack," she whispered. "Make love to me."

Eight

Without a word, Jack swept Annalise into his arms and carried her to the petal-strewn bed. He lowered her to the satin duvet, the rich ruby color a perfect complement to her hair and skin.

"Nudity becomes you, wife."

She laughed softly, just a hint of shyness evident in the deepening color that swept across her cheekbones. "I suspect it would become you, as well." She lifted an eyebrow. "Or were you going to make love to me with your pants on?"

Following her example, he removed his remaining clothing, lingering over the process the same way she had, despite the urgency to simply finish the job and get down to business. He wanted to go slow, to ease toward the moment when they became one. To build the memories one blistering touch at a time.

When he finished stripping, she moistened her lips and lifted up onto her elbows. "Jack…I think I should warn you that I've just started birth control but it's not effective yet. I guess I should have said something sooner."

"I'll take care of everything."

He made short work of the matter and then joined her on the bed. Candlelight flickered across her, gleaming on the sweet, rounded curves of her body and chasing darkness into the dips and valleys. He traced his index finger across the dusky tip of her breast, watching the nipple bead beneath the light caress.

"What should I do?" Annalise asked.

"Whatever you feel like. Nothing you do will be wrong."

"Show me how," she insisted. "Show me what you like."

Jack took her hands in his and guided them to his chest, pressed them there, close to his heart. Her fingertips danced across his flesh. Where once there was ice, each lingering stroke melted the coldness, turned it to warmth. Then to heat. He sank backward and gave himself up to her. Her undisguised pleasure and curiosity were a joy to witness. Little by little her inhibitions fell away and her stroking touch grew bolder.

She cupped him, then measured his length and width with her fingers and he closed his eyes, fighting to retain some vestige of control. This was a first for her, he reminded himself— her first memory of being with a man, of having free rein to indulge the sensuous side of her nature and explore to her heart's content—and he wanted it to be perfect. When she'd driven him as far as he could handle, he gathered her up and flipped her onto her back, caging her within his arms.

"Jack," Annalise whispered, her voice rife with emotion. "Make love to me."

He couldn't help but smile. "I'm working on it."

A soft laugh escaped. "Work faster."

Jack didn't listen. He took his time, not wanting to alarm her or do anything that might remind her of that long-ago event. He needn't have worried. With each touch she loosened, opening more and more of herself, both physically and emotionally. Shards of moonlight caught in her eyes, allowing him to witness her intense pleasure.

He cupped her breasts, filling his hands with the delicious weight of them while he teased the tips into excited buds. Then he tasted, reveling in the unique flavor of her. He felt the pounding of her heart against his cheek and the swift burst of her breath ruffling his hair. Sliding lower, he delved across the tensed muscles of her abdomen to the protected delta below. Cautiously, he drifted inward. Her small gasp of pleasure was all the encouragement he needed.

He pleasured her until he felt the early ripples of impending climax. Only then did he pull back and settle himself between her thighs.

Cupping her bottom, he lifted her and slowly surged inward. Her hips shifted to meet his, fighting to find the appropriate rhythm. It took her only a moment to discover it. And then instinct kicked in and she followed the beat. Moved with it. Drove it. Caught within her rapture, she was sheer radiance. She rode them toward a peak, further and higher than anything he'd thought possible. They teetered there for an endless moment before the first tiny convulsions shimmered through them. And then they shattered.

As he flew apart Jack realized that the cold had disappeared, replaced by a raging fire he didn't think could ever be doused. Annalise had done that to him. Had done that *for* him. Somehow, in some strange, unfathomable way, she'd freed him from the arctic wasteland in which he'd been living and brought him into the sun's balmy light.

* * *

"Are you all right?" Jack asked much, much later.

Annalise stirred against him. "I think so."

Her tentative comment alarmed him and he rolled over. Cupping her chin, he lifted it just enough so that the moonlight revealed her expression. Her mouth curved in a tremulous smile and a melting softness burnished her gaze. But he could also see a vague bewilderment that tautened her muscles and gave him a worrying sense of uneasiness.

"I'm sorry if it wasn't all you hoped it would be," he said. "It gets better with practice, I promise."

"I can't believe that's possible," she retorted with satisfying speed. She feathered a string of kisses across his chest. "That part was amazing. Incredible. And there's absolutely no comparison between last time and this."

Relief crashed over him. "I would hope not." He gathered up fistfuls of her hair so she had no choice but to look at him. "If that's not the problem, then what is?"

"It's not a problem, exactly."

"But…?"

She caught her lower lip between her teeth. For some reason the small gesture threatened to send him straight over the edge again. He wanted *his* teeth on that lip. Wanted to give it a small nip and tug. And then he wanted to soothe it, kiss it endlessly while he sank into her honeyed mouth. Before he could act, Annalise spoke again.

"Will it be like that every time?"

"Like that…good?" he asked cautiously.

"No, not good." His heart stopped in his chest, until she added, "That was incredible. That was amazing. That was…" She shook her head. "That was beyond belief. I had no idea. None."

"Your previous experience isn't a fair basis for comparison," he explained gently. He waited for her to absorb that. Once she did, his smile turned wicked. "In my opinion, we need more practice in order to improve."

Her eyes widened. "Improve? On *that?*" She lit up. "Are you serious?"

He didn't bother to respond. There was a far more satisfying way to answer her question. He applied himself to the task with all due diligence. He was going to enjoy married life, he decided. He was going to enjoy married life a *lot.*

The next few weeks passed in a blissful haze, overflowing with days of constant laughter, a heartwarmingly joyous Isabella and a fat and sassy Madam. And the nights were even fuller, each moment spent in Annalise's arms richer and more life-affirming than the one before. The changes served to solidify Jack's certainty that he'd done the right thing, both for his niece as well as for himself. Even Mrs. Locke cooperated, delaying her final visit so that the new family had an opportunity to settle into a comfortable routine.

Though Annalise continued to fuss because her father remained out of touch and she'd been unable to tell him about their marriage, Jack's father had given his opinion in no uncertain terms.

"Have you lost your mind?" Jonathan Mason demanded. "You married your nanny? What were you thinking?"

"Wasn't your second wife the au pair of one of your business associates?" Jack shot back. "Or was that wife number three? To be honest, I've lost track."

"I believe she was my third mistake," his father retorted. "I paid through the nose to escape that noose. At least tell me you had that woman sign a prenuptial agreement."

Defensiveness swept through Jack without thought or intention, an instinctive reaction to what he perceived on a gut level as an attack on one of his. His employee. His nanny. *His wife.* He couldn't explain when Annalise had come to mean so much to him, or even why. It wasn't their marriage alone, or the fact that she now shared his bed. It was more than that. Little by little she'd eased past his barriers and infiltrated every aspect of his life. Warmed it. Healed it. She wasn't just his employee, despite what their prenup might say. She was his wife, and he would defend her against everyone and everything, including his father.

"*That woman* has a name. She's Annalise Mason," Jack replied in a hard voice. "And you will treat her with the respect my wife deserves. Are we clear?"

To his surprise, his father apologized. "Call me once the two of you are past the honeymoon period. Suze and I will have you over for dinner. And, Jack…?" He paused, his hesitation out of character for a man so decisive. "One of the few comforts I've had these past few months is knowing that Joanne and I were able to rebuild our relationship before she died. I made a lot of mistakes when you were young. Terrible mistakes that I'd give anything to undo. Would you be willing… Do you think we—" He broke off abruptly.

Jack forced himself to pick up the ball. "Could start over?"

There was another long pause, and then: "I know I don't deserve it," Jonathan said in a rough undertone. "But I want to have my son and granddaughter in my life again. Your wife, as well, if you're willing."

For some reason, picturing Annalise's face stayed Jack's cold refusal. She would want him to take the proffered olive branch, as would Joanne. If his father could humble his pride—something Jack would have once thought an impossibility—so could he. "I'd like that, Dad. We'll call you and set a date."

"Thanks, Jack." Uncharacteristic emotion trembled in Jonathan's voice. "Anytime you're free. Anytime at all will be fine with us."

The weeks flowed by after that, and Family Bed became a Sunday morning staple. Little by little they accumulated furnishings that would better accommodate both a five-year-old and a massive klutz of a dog. Madam, in particular, reveled in her new home, her coat gleaming with health, while the regular nutritional meals kept her nicely filled out.

Or so he thought until Isabella woke them in the early morning hours with a piercing shriek. He was out of bed a split second before Annalise and raced flat out toward his niece's bedroom. She wasn't there. The covers of her bed were thrown back and Isabella was nowhere to be seen. Jack's heart began to pound in dread.

"Where is she?" Annalise said, slamming into him as she darted into the room. "What's happened?"

Her question was answered by another scream, coming from the direction of the playroom. The two of them flew down the hallway. It took him a minute to find his niece. He finally discovered Isabella and Madam inside the giant playhouse that occupied one end of the room. The dog lay on her side, straining, while his niece frantically petted her. She raised a tear-stained face to Jack and held out her arms. He scooped her up, checking her desperately for any sign of injury.

"What's wrong, Baby Belle?" he murmured. "Where are you hurt?"

"Jack, it's not Isabella. It's Madam. Look." A wet bundle of fur was tucked close to the dog. Madam licked the pup clean and nosed it toward her belly where it latched onto a nipple. Annalise stooped beside Jack and Isabella. "Don't cry, Isabella. Madam isn't hurt. She's having babies."

The change in his niece was instantaneous. Her eyes grew huge and a brilliant smile lit her face. She gave a little bounce that Jack swiftly stilled. "We need to be quiet. It's a lot of hard work to have puppies."

"I guess this explains why she was putting on so much weight," Annalise murmured, as Madam whelped another pup.

"It never occurred to me to ask the vet if she'd been spayed," Jack replied. "We'll get that taken care of as soon as the pups are weaned."

Over the next several hours, six puppies made their way into the world while Isabella looked on, wide-eyed and trembling with happiness.

"What are we going to do with all these dogs?" Annalise asked in dismay. "One Madam is wonderful. But six more…"

"Six more Madam-sized dogs are impossible, especially if these little guys are as klutzy as their mother." He released a gusty sigh. "I'll put the word out. We'll find good homes for them."

Isabella yanked on his arm, shaking her head.

"You want to keep them all, don't you, sweetie?"

She nodded emphatically.

He hesitated, wondering how he could explain it in terms she'd understand. "Do you remember your mommy and daddy telling you about the day they adopted you?" He could tell from her expression that she did. "They adopted you because the lady who gave birth to you…like Madam gave birth to all

these puppies…couldn't take care of you,
even though I'm sure she wanted to. Your
birth mommy did a wonderful thing. She
found someone who would love you and give
you a safe home because she wasn't able to.
In a few weeks, when these puppies are ready
to be out on their own, Madam won't be able
to take care of so many. It's our job to find
good mommies and daddies for all of
Madam's puppies, people who will love them
and keep them safe. Families with children
like you who need their own Madam. Do you
understand?"

He could tell Isabella wasn't happy about it, but
she nodded reluctantly. He tossed a relieved smile
over his shoulder in Annalise's direction, shocked
to see the tears streaking down her cheeks.

Fortunately, Isabella was so preoccupied with
the puppies, she didn't notice. With an inarticulate murmur, Annalise escaped the intimate
circle and distanced herself from them. Jack
followed. Some instinct warned that his wife

was hanging on by a mere thread, and, without a word, he pulled her into his arms.

"Honey, what's wrong?"

She simply shook her head without responding.

To his relief, Sara and Brett chose that moment to show up. They took in the situation in one glance. "Got a mite worried when no one appeared for breakfast." Sara spoke in an undertone. "Brett had a strong suspicion about what was going on. Mentioned just last night that Madam looked a bit plumper than a few weeks of decent meals could explain."

"I was going to give you the heads-up today," Brett added. "But I see Madam decided to break the news to you herself."

"That she did. Maybe if I'd had more experience with dogs I'd have caught on sooner." Jack spared his wife a swift glance. She continued to cling to him, her face buried in his shoulder. "Would the two of you mind keeping an eye on Isabella? Annalise isn't feeling well and I'd like to take her back to bed."

"Oh, dear," Sara said in concern. "Would it help if I fixed a pot of tea or a bite of toast?"

"I'll let you know," Jack assured. "I suspect Isabella will stay glued to Madam's side for the next few hours, so I don't think she'll be any trouble. Call on the house phone if you need me."

With that, he wrapped an arm around Annalise's waist and ushered her from the room. The second they entered the master suite, she turned and curled into him. His arms closed around her, holding her tight. He felt the shudders ripping through her and caught the small gasping sounds. He waited out the storm, trying to pinpoint what had set her off. Something about the birth of the dogs was all he could come up with.

At long last, she pulled free of his hold. "You can let me go now," she insisted. "I'm sorry to cause such a ridiculous scene."

He tipped up her chin and regarded her in naked concern. "Tell me what's wrong. Is it the puppies? Did they stir old memories of some kind?"

She waved that aside. "Not exactly. I don't know why I reacted in such a silly way. What you told Isabella…" She gave an embarrassed shrug. "I'm sorry. For some reason, it made me cry."

Aw, hell. "You do understand that we can't keep the puppies?" Just the thought of six more dogs as large as Madam rampaging through the house left him weak at the knees. "We can't give that many dogs the time and attention they deserve. We'd be doing them a disservice."

She lifted her tear-streaked face to his. "No, no. I understand that part."

"I'll find good homes for them. The best. I have a lot of contacts in both the local community and the business world. We'll find people whose homes and lifestyles are well suited for a large dog."

"I know you will. It's not that."

Another possibility occurred to him. "Was it what I said about Isabella's adoption?" he asked uneasily. "Joanne and Paul were very open with her about the subject, very matter-of-fact about it. They wanted her to understand the truth from an early age so there wouldn't be any unpleasant shocks later on in life. Not that they were cold-blooded about it," he hastened to add. "They were two of the most loving individuals I've ever known, and their daughter was at the center of that love."

"Everything that's happened to her just seems so unfair."

He hadn't quite gotten to the root of the problem and found himself floundering a bit in his attempt to pin it down. "That won't be an issue for her anymore," he reassured. "Not now that she has the two of us."

"But what about Mrs. Locke and CPS?"

Jack lifted Annalise's face and thumbed the remaining traces of tears from her cheeks. "They don't stand a chance against us."

A smile splashed across her face like sunshine following a cloudburst. It brightened her eyes, banishing the darkness. "How could I forget? You're Jack Mason. No one can stop a Mason once he makes up his mind to accomplish something."

He leaned in until they were almost nose to nose. "In case you've forgotten, you're a Mason now, too."

Her smile faded. "A temporary Mason," she corrected softly.

That did it. He caught hold of the lapels of her robe and reeled her in. Her warmth collided with his, her soft curves locking with stunning perfection against his hard-cut angles. He released her robe and sank his fingers into the mass of inky ringlets spilling down her back. They wrapped around him in joyous abandon, allowing him to anchor her close.

"Did it feel temporary last night when we made love?" he demanded. "Does it feel temporary when you're in my arms like this?"

He could read her uncertainty. "You know that's not what we agreed—" she began.

His mouth tightened. "I'm changing the terms of our agreement."

He didn't give her an opportunity to reply, stopping the incipient argument with a kiss. He kissed her with a passion that had little to do with Isabella and everything to do with his own selfish desires. Her reaction was instantaneous. She returned his embrace with an urgency that stole every thought but one. To lose himself in her. To join them in a way that would defy any and all attempts to force them apart. To bind and blend and mate one unto the other until two became one.

She must have felt something similar because she looked up at him and the longing in her eyes nearly unmanned him. "Please, Jack. Make love to me."

A final rational thought kept him from doing just that. "You're exhausted."

She shook her head. "Not that exhausted. Never that exhausted."

He couldn't resist. In all honesty, he didn't want to. He tugged at the belt anchoring her robe. It parted, revealing the paper-thin nightgown beneath. A brush of his hands sent the robe fluttering around their feet in a pool of vibrant aqua silk. Next he captured the two straps of her nightgown and drew them down her shoulders, baring her desire as he bared her. His clothing followed until all that remained between them was pure desire, a white-hot blaze that drove them toward the bed.

She sank into the mattress and lifted her arms to him, offering herself like some pagan goddess. He didn't hesitate. He claimed what she gave so willingly, branding her with his weight and desperate urgency. He found her breasts and claimed those as well, teasing them to rigidness with his teeth and tongue. Her arms enfolded him, pulling him closer still. And he sank into her heat, feeling the lap of it surround him, hearing the roar of it burning in his ears.

"I need this. I don't think I can survive without it. Not anymore."

"I'm here," she whispered in her siren's song. "I'm not going anywhere."

"No, you're not." Somehow it didn't come out as an agreement, but more as a warning. "You're mine now, and I protect and hold what's mine."

Amusement glittered in her witch gold eyes. "We're not possessive, are we?"

"Only with some things." He swept a hand from breast to thigh. *Mine,* his touch seemed to say. He couldn't seem to help it, his need to cleave to her had grown beyond his capacity to control. He tried to explain how he felt, fumbling over the unfamiliar words. "Now that I've found you, I don't want to lose you. Now that I've had you, I don't think I can go back to how it was before you were part of my life."

"Then don't."

There was so much more he longed to say. To explain. But he no longer possessed the ability. So he told her without words. He knew what she liked, what brought her the most pleasure. And he gave it to her. Each caress built, one on the other, and she clung to him as though she'd never let him go.

She trembled beneath his questing hand—the elegant line of her spine, the velveteen swell of her breast, the sweet curve of her thigh. He cupped the downy center of her passion, feeling the gathering tension and delicate quaking of a woman teetering on the verge. He drew her legs around his waist and drove slowly into her, losing himself in the delicious warmth. Her sigh of pleasure slid over him, sank deep inside to the very core of him, to that final place of coldness. With each ebb and flow, they moved ever closer. The eruption came, more powerful and overwhelming than any before.

He took her. Made her his. Let go of the final fragments of his control. When he did, the last sliver of ice melted. And in its place came love, a love he'd never anticipated or asked for. Never even thought possible.

But come it did.

Nine

Naturally, Mrs. Locke chose the worst possible time to arrive on their doorstep, descending six weeks after the birth of the puppies.

The morning started out perfectly, with Annalise in his arms still soft and trembling from the aftermath of their lovemaking. She wrapped him up in a tangle of arms and legs that held him close to the urgent beat of her heart. Though she never actually said the words, every lingering touch, every golden look, every whispered sigh, spoke of love.

Somehow she'd created a magical circle, a bountiful place more comfortable and spacious and exquisite than all the rooms in his family home combined. And in that circle she'd seeded a fertile garden where Isabella thrived. It was a place where he could loosen his grip on the chains of his restraint and reserve and simply let go. In that magical place, Madam romped and Isabella would soon speak and he belonged as he'd never belonged before.

For the first time, Jack felt hope. For the first time in more years than he could count, he'd found his way home, and he had no intention of ever losing his way again. He thrust his fingers deep into Annalise's silken curls and combed them back from her face. She smiled up at him, the words he longed to hear glittering in the brilliance of her eyes and trembling on the rose-petal softness of her lips, hovering so close he could practically hear the whisper of them on each exhalation of her breath. And yet, they remained unspoken.

It was time to take matters into his own hands.

"I want to change the parameters of our agreement," he stated bluntly.

Confusion clouded her gaze and a wariness settled over her. "You what?"

"I want to fire you."

She shoved at his chest and sat up, snatching the sheet to her chest. "Fire me," she repeated in patent disbelief. "Have you lost your mind? What about Isabella? What about CPS?"

His mouth set into a stubborn line. He reached beneath the covers and caught one silken bare leg. He gave it a sharp tug, sending her sliding back under him. "I want our marriage to be real. I want a wife. A permanent one, not a temp who's going to leave us in two years. Isabella needs a mother, and not any mother. She needs you."

For a brief instant she burned with happiness. The next instant it winked out of existence. "I can't promise you that," she stated categorically.

Had he misread her feelings? A rare panic swept through him and he clamped down on it, replacing it with every bit of strength and business acumen that he typically brought to the table whenever a deal threatened to go sour. He could handle Annalise. He'd handle her the same way he handled an unruly business transaction. He'd devastate her defenses with logic, boxing her in until she had nowhere to go other than straight into his arms.

"What's wrong with making our marriage a real one?" he demanded. "Aren't you happy?"

"I'm happier than I've ever been in my life," she conceded. "But our relationship is still new and untested. You don't know everything about me."

He settled on top of her, pressing her into the mattress. "That's the nice part about marriage. You have all those years to spend unwrapping each and every layer."

If anything his comment alarmed her even more. So much for boxing her in. One glimpse of the opening and she shied away. "What if you don't like what you find when all the wrapping paper's off?"

Was she kidding? "That's not possible," he stated quite definitely.

"Yes, Jack. It is." She moistened her lips and he could see her agile mind marshalling her counterarguments. What he didn't understand was why she found it necessary. "What happens if CPS decides to remove Isabella?"

Did she have any doubt? "We fight to get her back," he answered promptly. "To prove to them—no matter how long it takes—that we love her and will do whatever we must to give her the best possible home."

A small frown formed between her brows. "I mean… What happens to us? The entire reason we married was to provide your niece with a stable home. But what happens to our marriage if Isabella isn't in the picture?"

"Do you think I'll stop wanting you?"

"Yes," she replied bluntly.

He shook his head. "That won't happen."

Her breath caught and she searched his face. "Are you serious? If they took Isabella away, you'd want our marriage to continue?"

"Isn't that what you want, too?"

He could see the naked longing in her gaze, but it was tempered with caution…and something else. Something that had haunted her from the first time they'd met. Before she could reply, the door banged open and Isabella charged into the room with Madam. A tumble of puppies followed close behind. Jack glanced over his shoulder and stopped the entire menagerie in their tracks.

"That is not the proper way to enter a bedroom," he informed her in no uncertain terms. "Please take Madam and the puppies and go outside. Knock on the door and wait until you're invited in before opening the door. Got it?"

His niece stood there, debating whether to turn stubborn or to obey. To his relief, she spun around and shoved at Madam until the dog trotted out of the room. Then she herded the puppies. The instant the door shut behind them, Jack escaped the bed and tossed a nightgown in Annalise's direction while he donned a pair of drawstring pants.

"I believe you still owe me an answer to my question," he reminded his wife.

"There's no time to discuss it right now," she informed him.

"Tonight, then?"

She worried at that for a minute before releasing a gusty sigh and nodding. "Okay, fine. We'll talk about it again tonight."

For some reason, she didn't look happy about it, and a wintry coldness swept through him. He didn't know what secrets she kept, but he refused to lose the world she'd built for all of them. He wouldn't be forced from paradise now that he'd finally found it.

A soft knock sounded at the door of the bedroom, putting an end to the conversation. He opened the door to Isabella who, much to his delight, threw herself into his arms. Madam followed with matronly dignity, which the barking, squabbling puppies spoiled by nipping at her heels and jumping at her tail.

In the six weeks since their birth, they'd put on size and weight at an impressive rate. The vet had been very pleased with their progress during their last checkup and pronounced dame and puppies in excellent health. Jack had already promised three of the pups to eager families of business associates, and he doubted he'd have much difficulty placing the others. He hadn't told Isabella or Annalise, yet, but he'd already decided that they were going to keep the smallest of the six, a male who made up for his status as runt with a personality bigger than the other five combined. This one, in particular, had won all their hearts. He would also make a good companion dog for Madam.

The next hour passed in a rush as everyone pitched in to gather up the puppies and return them to the room in which they remained penned whenever they couldn't be watched. After dressing, he, Annalise and Isabella shared their ritual family breakfast before he headed off to the office. If a hint of stiltedness existed between husband and wife, it couldn't be helped. Whatever the cause, tonight would correct the situation. The instant they finished eating, his niece gave him a farewell kiss then made a beeline for the stairs leading to the bedrooms…and the dogs.

Jack turned to Annalise and held her gaze, forcing himself to use a hint of the ferocity that had helped him turn a small, startup import/export business into a multi-billion-dollar international success story. He aimed it straight in the direction of a lanky, golden-eyed ex-nanny with intoxicating kisses and a heart even larger than his bank account.

"Tonight," he reminded his wife. "Cards on the table." He didn't phrase it as a question.

She gave a steadfast nod. "I told you we would. But, Jack—" Her voice held an unmistakable warning. "You might not like the hand I deal you."

The doorbell sounded in the distance and his mouth twisted. "I may surprise you."

He dropped a swift kiss on his wife's mouth before going to answer the imperious summons. He opened the door, less than pleased to discover the Wicked Witch of all four compass points, plus several in between standing on his welcome mat. Or in her case, his unwelcome mat.

"Mrs. Locke."

"Mr. Mason."

He planted himself between her and his home and eyed the birdlike woman. He'd learned during their first meeting just how deceptive appearances could be. She barely reached the middle of his chest and appeared fragile enough for an errant breeze to snap in two. But that was as much a lie as the cheerful, robin's-egg-blue eyes that blinked sweetly from behind the lenses of her rimless spectacles. She offered a wide, guileless smile that didn't fool him for one little minute. She was a witch cloaked in the plumage of an innocent sparrow.

The two squared off against each other and Jack launched the first volley. "Did we have an appointment you forgot to arrange?" he asked mildly.

She looked entirely too pleased with herself which put him on instant alert. "It's called an unannounced home inspection."

"That's funny. According to my lawyer, you were supposed to call and arrange a convenient time for a visit."

"That would have defeated the entire point of the 'unannounced' portion of the inspection." She folded her twig arms across her nonexistent bosom. "Are you going to let me in, or are you going to continue looming there in that threatening manner?"

He narrowed his eyes at her phrasing. She narrowed hers right back at him. He wasn't sure how the stalemate might have ended if it hadn't been for Isabella charging toward him with a shriek. Her fingers fluttered in a gesture she used to alert them to a problem with the puppies. Then she yanked on his suit coat.

He turned to Mrs. Locke. "You'll have to leave. We have an emergency on our hands. That takes precedence over everything else."

She stiffened and yanked out a cell phone from the purse tucked beneath her arm with impressive speed. "Shall I call 9-1-1?" she asked crisply.

"That won't be necessary. It's a—" he hesitated "—dog emergency."

Mrs. Locke's brows climbed skyward. "A dog emergency is not an emergency I recognize," she informed him in a wintry tone. "The inspection will continue."

Isabella yanked harder at his suit coat and he rested his hand on her head in gentle reassurance. Damn it to hell. Why now, of all days? He regarded Mrs. Locke with a sour expression and gave her two options. "In that case, you may wait here until I'm available, or grace us with your presence at a more convenient time."

"I'll stay," she stated in tones as implacable as his own.

"Jack? Red alert. The puppies are on the loose." Annalise charged into the hallway and skidded to a halt. "Oh, we have guests."

Jack grimaced. This grew more complicated by the minute. He'd wanted time to prep Annalise before the two women met. "Mrs. Locke is *not* a guest. She's here for an inspection."

"Mrs. Locke?" To his disgust a broad, welcoming smile swept across his wife's face. "Isabella's Mrs. Locke?"

The caseworker inclined her head. "And I assume you're Mrs. Mason?"

"Oh, please. Call me Annalise." She held out her hand. "I'm afraid we have a bit of a family emergency going on here."

"So, I understand. Something to do with dogs?"

Isabella made a frantic noise and Jack interrupted. "Which we need to take care of immediately. Annalise, ask Sara and Brett to scour the first floor. I'll take the bedrooms. You and Isabella see if anyone's found their way to the third level. Since this isn't a scheduled appointment, Mrs. Locke can return at a more convenient time."

His beautiful, sexy, loyal wife fluttered her lashes at him and turned traitor in the blink of an eye. "I'll give Sara and Brett the heads-up while you and Isabella check the bedrooms. Mrs. Locke and I will be having some iced tea out on the patio. Once everyone's rounded up, you can join us there."

"Excellent suggestion," Mrs. Locked concurred. "I wanted some private time with your wife, anyway."

"I— You—"

Annalise smiled in satisfaction. "It's a plan. I'll call your office and warn them you're running behind." She fished her cell phone out of her pocket and hit a preprogrammed button. "Mary, it's Annalise. Jack's going to be late again. What? Oh, yes, of course. The pups on their usual rampage. Expect him when you see him."

Isabella didn't give him an opportunity to argue further. Grabbing his hand, she literally towed him in the direction of the steps. The last view he had of his double-crossing wife was her saucy backside vanishing in the direction of the kitchen, accompanied by the smirking Wicked Witch, her broomstick slung over one shoulder.

This was not good. Not good at all. He'd planned to be there the first time Annalise and Locke spoke, to run interference in case they hit any snags. Based on the smug look the case-worker shot him, she'd known it and took great delight in outmaneuvering him. Not that she'd actually been the one to make mincemeat of his plan. He could lay that delightful screwup squarely on his wife.

It took thirty nerve-racking minutes to round up five of the mischievous puppies and return them to the gated bedroom that was their "nest." Isabella remained with them while he went in search of the last one, the runt of the litter. He found Mister Mayhem, as he'd begun to refer to the dog, on the verge of sneaking out the kitchen door. He scooped up the wriggling bundle of energy before the pup could make good his escape.

From the direction of the patio, he caught the distinctive sound of feminine laughter. He stood there, literally frozen in disbelief. That couldn't possibly be Mrs. Locke laughing. Not the witch herself. He had no idea how Annalise managed to charm the woman, but he could only thank God it had happened. Then he immediately shook his head.

He did know how his wife had pulled it off. He'd watched her do it with him and Isabella, and every other person she met. She had a knack about her, a natural charm. No, even that wasn't quite right. She welcomed people in. Even though she'd been hurt, she hadn't allowed past events to close her down the way he had. She continued to open herself to others, despite the fact that she might get hurt again. The vulnerability remained, reflected in those magnificent eyes of hers. But she gave of herself, anyway.

The laughter had faded and he heard Mrs. Locke say, "So, tell me the truth, Annalise. Why did you marry your husband?"

Jack didn't think he could have moved if Doomsday itself were unfolding at his feet. Everything within him strained to hear the answer. But when it came, it was spoken so softly he couldn't catch the words he longed to hear.

He erupted from the kitchen onto the patio, the pup still cradled in his hands. He didn't know what he'd hoped, perhaps to discover Annalise's response still lingering on the summer breeze. Maybe to read it in her expression or glittering like gold dust in her eyes. Instead, her head swiveled in his direction and she simply smiled. Just that. A smile that made his heart stand still and left him more helpless and out of control than he'd ever been in his entire life.

"I assume that's the last straggler? Mayhem?"

she asked. "Isn't that what you've dubbed him?"

"Mister Mayhem," he muttered.

"Would you like a glass of sweetened tea?"

The prosaic question ripped him to shreds. It took every ounce of willpower to hold himself in check, when what he wanted more than anything was to tip Locke out of his patio chair and chuck her onto the street so that he could demand his wife repeat to him whatever she'd told the caseworker. He wanted—*needed*—to hear why she'd married him. To know once and for all whether she'd done it just for Isabella or if maybe, just maybe, she'd believed those vows she'd spoken right here in his backyard.

To love, honor and cherish…

Annalise tilted her head to one side and a wealth of curls tumbled across her shoulder. "Tea?" she prompted again in open amusement.

"Thanks, I'd love some." He crossed to her side and dropped a kiss on the top of her head. "Everything okay?"

"Everything's fine."

He took a seat with Mayhem in his lap and tipped the dog onto his back. He rubbed the puppy's plump belly with his index finger. With a wide yawn, Mayhem promptly went to sleep, his head, tail and legs splayed in six different directions.

He glared across the table at Mrs. Locke. "Have you finished interrogating my wife?" he asked.

He knew he sounded defensive, just as he had with his father. But this time he had cause. He had it figured out now. This woman wasn't his niece's nanny any more than she was his employee. Annalise was his wife, a woman who'd given herself to him in marriage. Given herself in every way possible. And he'd do everything within his power to protect her, to fulfill those vows he'd taken mere steps from where they sat.

"I just put away my thumbscrews," she replied in a dry voice. "And now I have one final question before I go visit with Isabella."

He regarded her warily. "Only one?"

"Just one." She leaned forward and set her glass of tea onto the patio table. "I know why Annalise married you. But I'd like you to explain why you married your wife. Is this a love match or is this your clever way of circumventing CPS's objections to your guardianship? Is Annalise here to stay, or here until we go away?"

And there it was, Jack acknowledged. The billion-dollar question.

Before he could reply, Sara stepped onto the patio. "Excuse me, Mr. Mason. There's a gentleman here to see you. He was most insistent—"

Not waiting for either permission or invitation, a tall, lean man in his late thirties, maybe early forties, strode out onto the patio. He carried himself with a military bearing. His curly brown hair was cropped short. A faded cap shaded his deep-set eyes and cast a shadow across his sun-bronzed face. Though he didn't

share Annalise's coloring and appeared far too
young to have a daughter his wife's age, there
was little doubt in Jack's mind that this had to
be her father—and his timing couldn't have
been worse.

"I'm Robert Stefano," he announced. "And
I'm looking for…" He froze, his eyes arrowing
in on Annalise. "Leese?"

"Daddy?" Annalise erupted from her chair
and threw herself into the man's arms. "Finally!
I have been trying to reach you for ages."

He gave his daughter a fierce hug. "Didn't
you get my message?"

"About your charter? Yes, yes. Bub passed
it on. But—"

He held her at arm's length. "I came as soon
as I heard the news. Of course, by the time it
reached me, it was long out of date. What the
hell have you gone and done?"

He looked over her shoulder toward Jack, who
climbed to his feet and set the yawning puppy
on the ground beside him. "It's a pleasure to

meet you, Mr. Stefano," he said, holding out his hand. "I'm Jack Mason."

To Jack's dismay, his father-in-law swept his daughter behind him in a protective manner. "Not him, Leese. Tell me there's been a mistake and you haven't actually married this man."

"Is there a problem?" Mrs. Locke interrupted.

"No problem at all," Jack replied smoothly. His hand dropped to his side. "You need to leave. Now. This is a family matter and none of your business."

Of course, she didn't listen. She settled more firmly into her chair. "If this affects Isabella, it most certainly is my business."

"Mr. Stefano?" Jack approached the other man. "I'm Annalise's husband."

"I know who you are." Robert tore off his cap and crushed it between his callused hands. "What I don't yet know is what sort of game you're playing with my daughter."

Annalise stepped out from behind her father, confronting the situation head-on, just as she had from the moment he'd first met her. "Dad, this isn't a game."

"You're damn right it isn't." Grief tore into the older man's face. "Does he know? Does this supposed husband of yours know the truth?"

To Jack's surprise she faltered, her forthright-ness stumbling. "No," she admitted. "He doesn't."

Dread swept through him like the first winter breeze. "Somebody tell me what the *hell* is going on," Jack demanded.

"And then you can explain it to me," Mrs. Locke added.

Robert opened his mouth to reply, but before he could his gaze shifted and locked onto something in the middle of the lawn. Mister Mayhem scampered in that direction and Jack saw why. Isabella had exited into the yard through his study door. She greeted the dog with a crowing laugh.

"Oh, God," Robert whispered. His cap dropped to the patio flagstones. "Is that her?"

He took a step in Isabella's direction, a step that carried him into the sunlight. The strong summer rays caught in the short brown curls, highlighting them with gold. He stared at Isabella, stared at her with eyes the exact same shade of olive green as those of Jack's niece. Robert clenched his squared jaw, but couldn't seem to keep it from wobbling. And then he broke into a broad grin of incandescent delight. In his cheek a dimple flashed.

Without a word, Jack turned toward Annalise. Tears rained down her cheeks. She caught his look, holding his eyes for an endless moment, hers assuming a defiant slant. He went to her, stepped with her into the shadows of the patio overhang, away from listening ears.

"Isabella looks just like your dad. Is she your sister?" Jack questioned in a hard undertone. "Is Robert Stefano her father?"

"I'm an only child," Annalise stated.

An arctic wind blew through him and he could literally see the life he'd built shattering around him. "Then she's—"

"Mine." Annalise squared her shoulders and lifted tarnished eyes to his. "Isabella is my daughter."

Ten

"It was all a setup, wasn't it?"

"No." Annalise shook her head, speaking with a quiet dignity that cut deep. "No!"

Jack stepped away from her, unable to hide his raw pain and anger. There was no way he could. His fury battered him with all the elemental power of a hurricane, driving emotions he'd always been able to keep under rigid control. They whipped free, exploded from him in a messy, illogical, unmanageable torrent.

"I have to hand it to you. Your plan was absolutely brilliant."

"What plan?" She played the role of the innocent with breathtaking perfection, reflecting just the appropriate amount of bewilderment. "All I ever wanted was to make certain Isabella was safe."

"Safe," he repeated. "I didn't realize my reputation was quite that bad."

She dared to fight back. "You know that's not what I meant."

He ignored that and continued the attack with ruthless precision. "Why did you apply to be Isabella's nanny? You knew she was yours then, didn't you?" He didn't phrase it as a question.

She lifted her chin, refusing to cower. "Yes."

"What then, Annalise? Were you going to use your position to manipulate CPS? To push them that final inch in order to convince them I wasn't an appropriate guardian?"

"Have you lost your mind?" she asked with impressive calm.

He simply shook his head, amazed by her inner fortitude. "I have to hand it to you. Your logic was flawless. As Isabella's nanny you could inveigle yourself into my niece's affections. Maybe drop a word or two of concern in Mrs. Locke's ear."

A spark of anger appeared, at war with her self-control. She folded her arms across her chest. "And then what, Jack? Have Isabella's life upended again when they put her into foster care? Or even worse, stick her into a treatment program?"

He lifted a shoulder in a negligent shrug. "Once she was out of my control you'd have a better shot at getting custody of her."

Fury blossomed, full-throttled and magnificent. "*That's* what you think this is all about? You think I want to take her away from you?"

His anger rose to meet hers. "What am I supposed to think? In all this time, never once did you bother to say, 'Oh, hey, Jack, just so you know, Isabella's my biological daughter.'" He stalked closer. "Did you think I'd never find out?"

"I was going to tell you!"

"Right. Now that we're safely married and you're in an even better position to fight for legal custody."

She went nose to nose with him. "Is that your real opinion of me? After all this time together, you don't know me better than that?"

The ache was almost more than he could bear. "I thought I did," he whispered. "But you lied."

"I never lied. I just didn't tell you all of it." She dared to splay her hand across his chest. Could she still feel his heart beating? It wasn't possible. Not when it had been turned to stone. "Would you have refused to marry me if I'd told you beforehand?"

"I don't know." The confession was ripped from him. "But at least I would have been in a position to make an informed choice."

Her hands dropped to her sides, stealing away the only warmth left to him. She stepped backward. "Then let me make this easy for you." She took another step away from him. "I'll narrow your choices down to two. We can stay married and work through this, or we can divorce."

"And if I want a divorce?"

For the first time, her composure cracked. No, it more than cracked. It shattered. He found that shattering all the more devastating because he'd never seen her lose control to that extent before. She fought the loss for ten full seconds before managing to grind out a reply. "When we first met I had serious doubts about whether or not you were the appropriate person to raise Isabella. I don't have any doubts about that anymore."

He froze. "What the hell does that mean?"

"I think you're an amazing father, Jack," she said. "There's not a single doubt in my mind that she'd not just be safe with you, but that she'll thrive in your care. I won't contest a divorce. Nor will I attempt to take her away from you."

"Annalise—"

She shook her head and her mouth compressed, he suspected to keep her lips from trembling. "If you change your mind about the divorce, you know where to find me." She squared her shoulders and looked him straight in the eye. "But if you decide you want to give our marriage a try, there's only one way I'll return to you. And that's not as Isabella's nanny or your employee. It will be as your partner. As your wife."

With that, Annalise turned and stepped into her father's arms. She clung to him for a long minute while Robert stared at Jack with eyes filled with threat. Without another word, he swept his daughter across the patio and into the house. There they paused, and her gaze clung to an oblivious Isabella a final instant. Not once did she look back at him. Then the door closed behind them with frightening finality.

Jack stood unmoving for an endless moment. How was it possible that in thirty short minutes his life had gone from near perfection, straight to hell? Isabella continued to play with Mister Mayhem, giggling in blissful ignorance at the puppy's ungainly antics. He took a single step toward her when a voice like shards of glass cut into him.

"You, Mr. Mason, are a complete and total idiot," Mrs. Locke announced in ringing tones of disgust.

He spun in his tracks. He'd completely forgotten about the caseworker. She continued to sit beneath the canopied portion of the patio. Without taking her gaze from him, she picked up her glass of iced tea with impressive casualness and took a dainty sip.

She offered a sour smile. "Forgot I was here, didn't you?" He muttered a word that had the woman's carefully stenciled eyebrows climbing. "I certainly hope you don't use that sort of language around Isabella on a regular basis," she said.

"Since she doesn't talk, I didn't think it mattered," he shot back.

To his amazement, Mrs. Locke actually smiled. "I suggest you come and sit down before you fall down." She hefted the pitcher of tea and splashed some into one of the empty glasses. "Here. Drink this."

He reluctantly approached, amazed to find himself taking the proffered glass and obediently downing half the contents in one swallow. The sugar rush hit his system and helped clear his head. "So, how's your morning been so far, Mrs. Locke?" He collapsed into the chair across from the caseworker and stared broodingly at his niece. "Entertaining enough for you?"

"Vastly."

"Glad you enjoyed yourself. Personally, the last time I had a day this bad I was told my sister and her husband had been killed on a flight I was supposed to have been on with them, and that my niece was hanging on to life by a mere thread."

"I'm sorry, Jack." There was no mistaking either her sincerity or her compassion.

He found he couldn't respond. Instead, he traced his finger along a teardrop bead of condensation trickling down the side of his glass. He struggled to gather himself and determine what his next step should be. Having built his business from scratch, he'd learned the importance of flexibility. He'd been an expert at thinking and organizing quickly, and reacting to fluid situations even faster. Logic and ruthless intent had gotten him through many a crisis. But this...

He couldn't think at all, let alone act.

"So, did you marry Annalise because you loved her, or in order to get rid of me?" Mrs. Locke asked.

"To get rid of you." He returned the glass to the table and rubbed at the headache gathering in his temples. "At least, I thought that was the reason."

"Interesting."

His head jerked up. "What's interesting?"

"When I asked Annalise why she'd married you, she said more or less the same thing."

He had a vivid memory of standing in the kitchen, desperate to hear his wife's response to Mrs. Locke's question. The truth came as one more blow. He didn't even attempt to conceal his pain. It cut too deeply. "She told you that?" he murmured.

"No, she told me that's why she'd initially agreed to marry you. She said she married you for one reason and one reason only."

"What?" The word was torn from him before he could prevent it.

Mrs. Locke lifted an eyebrow and pinned him with those bright blue eyes. "Don't you know?" She dismissed her own question with a wave of her hand. "Of course you don't, or you'd never have made those ridiculous accusations."

"Are you going to tell me what she said, or not?" he ground out.

"Not," came the crisp response. "To be honest, it doesn't matter what Annalise said. All that matters is what you have to say. Why did you marry your wife, Mr. Mason? I expect a truthful answer and I expect one now."

The question didn't require any thought. "Because I love her," he answered starkly.

Mrs. Locke pushed back her chair. "I'll give

you three days to resolve this situation before rendering my final verdict on Isabella's custody."

He lifted his gaze, feeling the protective predator stirring. No one was going to take his niece from him. "Is that a threat?" he asked softly.

Just like Annalise, Mrs. Locke didn't show the least sign of intimidation. What was it with these women? "Yes, Mr. Mason." She picked up her purse and tucked it under her arm. "That was a threat."

It didn't take three days for Jack to figure out what he intended to do. It didn't even take him three hours. It just took enough time for him to sit quietly and remember. Remember Annalise and how she'd been from the moment they'd first met. From the day she'd stepped foot in his office, she'd lived and breathed her concern for his niece.

No, not just his niece. *Annalise's daughter*.

She hadn't accepted the position of Isabella's nanny with the intent of attracting a wealthy husband. It hadn't been about him at all. All her attention, all her focus, had been directed toward Isabella and helping her child recover from a hideous trauma that had forever changed her young life.

Even by giving Isabella up for adoption, Annalise had proven that she'd put Isabella first and done what was best for his niece. Marrying him had simply been one more step in that process. He might have wanted her focus to widen enough to include him. But that wasn't her first priority and never would be. Her child was Annalise's priority. He closed his eyes.

Their child.

His gaze drifted to Isabella and he accepted the inescapable truth. She was his niece and he'd always keep her parent's memory alive for her. But at some point, he'd stopped thinking of her as an extension of Joanne and Paul, and begun to think of her as part of himself. A vital part.

As though sensing his attention, Isabella's

head jerked up and she looked at him and beamed with happiness. Sweeping Mister Mayhem into her arms, she trotted over to him and climbed into his lap. He hugged her close, inhaling the sweet, baby scent of her. From tragedy had come an existence he'd never believed possible.

It didn't matter what it took. It didn't matter what he had to sacrifice. It didn't even matter that he'd never be first in Annalise's life or heart. He and Isabella needed her and he'd do whatever necessary to bring his wife home. But there was something he had to do first.

He gathered Isabella close and prayed he'd find the right words. "Do you remember when we talked about finding people to adopt Madam's puppies, like you were adopted?" he asked.

Isabella nodded, though he could tell she still pouted a bit at the thought.

"Do you also remember me telling you about your other mommy? She's the one who gave birth to you before you were adopted?" When Isabella nodded again, he rested his cheek against the soft curls crowning her head. He gathered his self-control and spoke gently. Carefully. Lovingly. "There's something I need to tell you about your birth mommy…"

Jack arrived at the boatyard early that same afternoon. Sun pounded down on him as he walked the weathered planks toward the large charter yacht he'd been informed belonged to Robert Stefano. He saw Annalise's father before the other man caught sight of him. It gave Jack a few seconds to further assess the man and get some sort of handle on him.

Lean and muscular, Robert Stefano wore cutoff shorts and a sleeveless tee, which made him look all the younger and more virile than when he'd first introduced himself. He didn't wear a cap and the sun picked out the burnished streaks that were so similar to Isabella's. He must have realized that he was being watched.

His head jerked up and he stiffened, like one predator sensing the presence of another. Slowly, he swung around. Cursing roundly, he stalked down the pier, planting himself square in Jack's path. He folded his well-muscled arms across an equally muscular chest.

"What the hell are you doing here?" he demanded.

Jack assessed his opponent—who also happened to be his father-in-law. He could take the man if he had to. Maybe. He imitated Robert's stance. "I've come for my wife, even if I have to go through you to get to her. But when I leave, it's with Annalise. Now, I can do it with your cooperation, or without. Your choice."

"I vote for 'without.' She's not a real wife to you. She's just a means to an end, and I won't let you use her. So turn around, son." A vicious smile slashed across Robert's face. "You don't stand a chance against me. I eat pencil pushers like you for breakfast."

Jack planted himself, hoping for peace, but

prepared for the battle of his life. "Annalise tells me you raised her on your own after her mother died."

"I did." Open grief touched his tanned face before being ruthlessly suppressed. "I let that girl down when she was sixteen. I won't let her down now."

"Sounds like we have ourselves a problem, because I don't want to let Isabella down. She needs Annalise." He drew a deep breath and confessed, "*I* need Annalise."

Suspicion glinted in Robert's green eyes. "For your niece?"

Jack shook his head. "For me. It just took me a while to realize that. Isabella was the excuse I used to bind Annalise to me without admitting why I wanted her."

Robert's arms dropped to his sides and he cocked his head to one side in a gesture eerily similar to Annalise's. "And why is that?"

Jack didn't bother to pull his punches or hide behind his pride. He put it all out there for the other man to rummage through. "Because I love your daughter."

Robert eyed him for a long moment, before nodding in satisfaction. "Then what are you doing wasting your time jawing with me?" He stepped aside. "Go tell my daughter how you feel and put her out of her misery."

"I'll get right on that." Jack didn't hesitate. He passed by the other man and walked toward his future.

"Mason?" Robert waited until Jack turned. "That's two of mine in your care. I will be watching you."

Jack nodded. He could accept that. "I'd be doing the exact same thing if I were in your position." He swung aboard only to have Robert stop him again.

"Oh, and Mason?"

"Yes, sir?"

"You couldn't have taken me."

Jack grinned. "I would have enjoyed trying."

Robert returned the grin. "Yeah. Me, too."

A cursory glance told Jack that Annalise wasn't topside. He crossed the deck to the steps leading to the shadowed interior. His wife stood in the small, efficient galley, her back to him. He paused and allowed himself the luxury of watching her graceful movements as she went about the mundane task of putting a meal together.

She'd swept her hair into a casual ponytail, and the ringlets bounced with each dip and sway of her body. She wore a thin cotton tee that hugged her curves and screeched to a halt a scant couple of inches short of a pair of low-slung shorts that bared her endless legs to his view. He was about to announce his presence when she spoke without turning.

"I have your lunch ready, Dad. Grab a beer out of the fridge if you want one."

"I don't want a beer, thanks."

Her spine went rigid and she carefully returned the plate to the counter with hands that trembled. She drew a careful breath before spinning around. "Jack."

"Annalise."

One look warned that her control was as tenuous as his own. Unfortunately, he still couldn't read her as well as he'd hoped. *Why had she married him?* Was it just for Isabella, or was there more? He'd obsessed over the question ever since his conversation with Mrs. Locke. He wanted to be able to take one look and see the answer in her face. But it wasn't there, and unadulterated fear threatened to bring him to his knees.

"I've been expecting a call from Derek," she said. "I'm surprised you came, instead."

Gathering every shred of composure at his command, Jack leaned his hip against the counter and shrugged. "What's this got to do with Derek? You're *my* wife, not his."

Her chin assumed a combative angle. "For now."

"Forever," he stated decisively.

She shook her head. "Forget it, Jack. I won't live with someone who believes I'm capable of—"

"Stop." He cut her off with that one, quiet word. Perhaps it was the way he said it—naked pain leaking into the single syllable. Whatever the reason, it worked and she stumbled to a halt. "Please, sweetheart. You're killing me."

She gazed at him with a heartbreaking defenselessness that he recognized, mainly because he felt it, too. It was an emotion he'd never experienced before...until now. He'd always been the tough one. He'd always held himself at a safe distance, refusing to allow himself to feel or show the vulnerability she displayed so openly. And what had that gotten him? Money. Success. But what were those in comparison to an empty heart and a cold bed, and a little girl waiting for a mother? He'd had a taste of heaven, and he would do anything and everything to have that back.

Even strip his defenses bare and allow her to cut him to shreds.

Without a word, he opened his arms to her. Time seemed to hold its breath as he waited for her decision. Waited to discover whether he'd know a lifetime of warmth and joy, or be forced to survive in an arctic wasteland. With an inarticulate cry, she flew to him, and he breathed in life. He wrapped her up tight and buried his face against her silken curls and simply inhaled her. The scent of her. The feel of her. The sound of their hearts beating as one.

"I love you, Annalise," he murmured against the top of her head. "And I'm more sorry than I can ever express."

She lifted a glowing face to his. "Sorry you love me?" she teased.

A rusty laugh escaped. "I'm sorry I believed the worst."

"I should have told you about my relationship to Isabella. I was going to." She made a gesture that emphasized her bone-deep weariness. "But I should have done it before we married."

"Tell me now, Annalise. I gather Isabella was the result of that night you lost your virginity?"

"Yes." She closed her eyes and shuddered.

"You have no idea how terrified I was when I realized I was pregnant."

"What about the boy?"

"He and his family had moved away by then. Dad contacted them, of course. But they wanted nothing to do with me or the baby and were only too happy to sign the adoption papers." She shrugged. "It was just as well. Tommy was no more in a position to raise a baby than I was."

"I remember Joanne saying it was a private adoption, arranged through their lawyer."

Annalise nodded. "Dad met with Joanne and Paul and had them carefully checked out."

He eyed her curiously. "You never considered keeping Isabella?"

It was the wrong question to ask. Her chin wobbled for an instant before she firmed it. "I wanted to keep her with all my heart. I dreamed about it every night. But I was sixteen when I got pregnant. I'd just turned seventeen when I had her." The confession was so soft he barely caught it. "I also know it was the most difficult decision Dad ever made. He'd been a teenage father himself, and he felt he'd done such a poor job of it, that it wouldn't be fair to repeat the cycle for another generation. He was right. I couldn't be selfish." Tears overflowed. "I...I had to do what was best for Isabella, not what was best for me. So I hid my pregnancy until the school year ended and went to stay with my aunt until after Isabella was born. Every summer after that I'd go and stay with her...and remember. Celebrate...and mourn."

He tightened his hold on her, her words tearing him apart. "I'm so sorry."

"I never knew who adopted her, but Dad kept track and would reassure me that she was safe and doing well."

Understanding dawned. "Until the plane crash."

"Yes. It was all over the news. At first, the media reported that everyone onboard perished. I walked in while Dad was listening to the announcement. He was crying. He tried to keep it from me, but it wasn't hard to figure out why he was so upset."

"I gather you read that I'd taken custody of your daughter."

She nodded against his chest. "And that you were having a hard time keeping a nanny. It seemed the perfect opportunity. I'd apply and see if there was anything I could do to help with the transition. I planned to stay just a short time. Neither of you were supposed to discover the truth. I didn't even intend to tell my father I'd taken the job. But then…"

"Then?"

Her sigh rippled through her and into him. "I took one look at her and fell head over heels. I would have stuck to my original plan if it weren't for one other problem."

He stiffened. "What problem?" he managed to ask.

She lifted her head and looked at him, her heart in her eyes. "I fell in love with you. One minute I was trying to build a world for you and Isabella, and the next you became my world."

The inner coldness cracked, splitting apart like chunks of icebergs beneath a spring thaw. He didn't resist any longer. He lowered his head and kissed her. The kiss shouldn't have been any different from all the other ones they'd shared. But it was. He didn't know if it was the absence of secrets or the fact that they'd both allowed the last bastions of their defenses to fall. Maybe the fact that they'd confessed their love altered the elemental nature of the embrace. Whatever the cause, he knew he'd remember this moment for the rest of his life. Remember the heat and the generosity, the certainty and the passion. Most of all, it was the awareness that he'd finally come home. That he'd found what he'd spent most his life searching for—and he held her safely in his arms.

"Come home now," he urged. "We're lost without you."

"I thought I was the one who was lost."

He forked his hands deep into her hair, allowing the curls to bind them together. "The three of us ultimately found each other. That's all that matters now."

He took her mouth in a lingering kiss, sinking into the softness and the warmth. If they'd been anywhere else, he'd have fallen into the nearest bed and spent the next twenty-four hours making her his in every possible sense of the word. Reluctantly, he drew back.

"I never realized how empty my life was until you filled it up," he said.

Her smile was the most radiant he'd ever seen. "Let's go home."

Robert eyed them closely as they left the boat. Whatever he saw must have satisfied him because he simply smiled in satisfaction. "I'd appreciate having an opportunity to get to know my granddaughter," he addressed Jack. "If you're willing."

"Anytime."

The drive to Lover's Folly seemed endless. But they finally arrived. It felt like weeks since he'd last had his wife at home, instead of mere hours. They walked hand in hand from the garage across the backyard. The kitchen door flew open and a half dozen rambunctious puppies spilled out, yipping and squabbling as they came, with Madam close on their heels.

Behind them, Isabella appeared in the doorway and cut loose with a shriek to end all shrieks. She took off at a flat run and arrowed straight for Annalise. His wife released his hand and knelt, cushioning Isabella's landing in a loving embrace.

"Hello, Baby Belle," Annalise greeted her daughter with a tearful laugh.

Isabella twined her twig-thin arms around Annalise's neck and buried her face in the soft crook between neck and shoulder. Jack found he had to swallow hard at the sight. Isabella pulled back and spared him a brief, nervous glance. He gave an encouraging nod, praying for a miracle. And then it happened.

With a shy look, Isabella said, "Hi, Mommy."

* * * * *

millsandboon.co.uk Community

Join Us!

The Community is the perfect place to meet and chat to kindred spirits who love books and reading as much as you do, but it's also the place to:

- **Get the inside scoop from authors about their latest books**
- **Learn how to write a romance book with advice from our editors**
- **Help us to continue publishing the best in women's fiction**
- **Share your thoughts on the books we publish**
- **Befriend other users**

Forums: Interact with each other as well as authors, editors and a whole host of other users worldwide.

Blogs: Every registered community member has their own blog to tell the world what they're up to and what's on their mind.

Book Challenge: We're aiming to read 5,000 books and have joined forces with The Reading Agency in our inaugural Book Challenge.

Profile Page: Showcase yourself and keep a record of your recent community activity.

Social Networking: We've added buttons at the end of every post to share via digg, Facebook, Google, Yahoo, technorati and de.licio.us.

www.millsandboon.co.uk